Message
from a Ghost

Message from a Ghost

Marilyn Ross

Thorndike Press • Chivers Press
Thorndike, Maine USA   Bath, England

This Large Print edition is published by Thorndike Press, USA and by Chivers Press, England.

Published in 2001 in the U.S. by arrangement with Maureen Moran Agency.

Published in 2001 in the U.K. by arrangement with Marilyn Ross.

U.S. Hardcover 0-7862-3336-2 (Romance Series Edition)
U.K. Hardcover 0-7540-4542-0 (Chivers Large Print)

The text of this Large Print edition is unabridged.
Other aspects of the book may vary from the original edition.

Set in 16 pt. Plantin by Christina S. Huff.

Printed in the United States on permanent paper.

British Library Cataloguing-in-Publication Data available

Library of Congress Cataloging-in-Publication Data

Ross, Marilyn, 1912-
  Message from a ghost / Marilyn Ross.
    p. cm.
  ISBN 0-7862-3336-2 (lg. print : hc : alk. paper)
  1. Sisters — Fiction. 2. Inheritance and succession —
Fiction. 3. Fathers and daughters — Fiction.
  4. Seances — Fiction. 5. Large type books. I. Title.
PR9199.3.R5996 M47 2001
  813'.54—dc21   2001023532

To my good friend GEORGE MARSHALL, one of Boston's fine orchestra leaders, and his excellent group, especially George Briggs.

With memories of the Marshall House, July 1971 and the writing of *House of Dark Shadows*.

Chapter One

The skull floated in the grimy yellow light, its dark, empty eyesockets grim and accusing above the fixed smile of its bared teeth. Then it swooped down — so close that the gray coarseness of its high cheekbones was plainly visible. There was a shrill scream of laughter and the skull vanished. A wistful Harlequin mask, with red nose and large ruby lips and forlorn eyes accented with black arrows, took its place. And as soon as this grotesque face vanished, an evil Svengali countenance came swooping from the shadows, hook-nosed, malevolent-eyed, and with a scraggy black beard on a pointed chin. It loomed there in the uncertain light and the weird laughter came loudly again!

Gale Garvis shrank back from the horror suspended above her with piteous fear showing in her lovely blue eyes. Since she had come to this place of terror she had changed from a bright, pretty twenty-two year old girl athlete to a frightened, dishevelled creature on the edge of a complete breakdown. Her long yellow hair was matted and dirty and her pert, oval face was smudged. Her chic green linen dress was torn in several places and begrimed.

Staring up at the leering, bestial mask floating above her as she crouched on the floor in the corner of the small dressing room, she couldn't be sure whether this was a period of reality or another of her blackouts. Sometimes she had trouble determining which was which. And she was sure that was what they wanted. Not satisfied to have her merely a prisoner, they sought complete control of her mind and body.

Clenching her fists, she fought to keep her thoughts rational. She was a prisoner of these people for no reason she understood, kept against her will in this deserted, cavernous old movie palace, tormented by the weird creatures hired to carry out the task of being her jailers. The mad laughter echoing above her now was a sharp reminder of her plight.

Glancing up, she saw the small ugly face of the midget, Harry, as he danced back and forth on the make-up shelf on the opposite wall of the narrow dressing room, dangling the masks he'd lifted from a nearby hook and swinging them out at her so they seemed menacing ghost faces!

In his shrill, piping voice he cried out, "Don't you like the phantoms? They were here in this old theatre long before you!"

"Stop!" she pleaded, her face anguished.

The tiny three-foot creature on the shelf chortled with glee. He was old. His wrinkled, sallow face and white hair and the heavy bags under his eyes testified to that. But his body was the size of a five year old's. He wore a shabby gray suit, and a jaunty brown beret covered his bald head. In her captivity Harry had been her chief torturer. She knew him to be thirty-six inches of sheer menace. Hatred oozed from him.

He tossed the masks aside and stepped down from the shelf onto a plain wooden chair and then from it he carefully backed down to the floor using the chair rung as a ladder. Now he was at her level and he came over to her.

"Solon is coming today," he gloated, his ugly little face showing a nasty smile.

The name conjured up a vision of a silent, frightening hawk of a man with a harsh voice, whose curt instructions were always carried out by the weird group who held her captive. From the first moment she'd seen him, she'd felt a chill of fear rush through her, had sensed the evil in his presence. But that had been long ago, she thought wearily, before she'd been caught up in this nightmare!

The midget thrust a tiny forefinger in her

face and warned her, "Solon has plans for you! You know that, don't you?"

"I don't know anything!" she replied in distress. "Not why I'm being kept here or why you delight in torturing me!"

Harry smiled nastily. "It's part of my job. And I always do my work well. When I was call boy here in this old theatre I was always prompt in knocking on the doors. 'Five minutes, miss,' I'd say, or 'Curtain going up.' I was always on time. And now it's a ghost comes knocking on these doors!"

"I don't want to hear about it," she said, bowing her head, still crouching dejectedly on the floor.

He chuckled. "You'll see her one of these nights. The ghost is bound to call on you. Just as she's called on the rest of us."

She raised her head and gave him a pleading look. "Why don't you let me escape? I've done you no harm! Why do you help them keep me here?"

Harry's lined face showed a look of hate. "Because all my life I've been looked down on by beauties like you. It pleases me to think that one of you is going to suffer for the lot. You'll know what it is to become a freak! Solon has plans for you! Don't you forget it!" And he laughed again in his shrill, mad fashion.

Gale's head was swirling. She felt really ill. Clinging to reality was becoming more difficult. Had they put a mind-blasting drug in her food or drink? Lately she had faded in and out of reality without being able to surely separate one from the other. But this had to be real!

She stared at Harry's ugly, grinning face in the murky yellow glow of the single bare bulb suspended from the ceiling of the long, narrow dressing room. The cubicle was one of a row under the stage of the ancient movie palace. Fleeing from the midget, she had sought refuge in the dressing room. But he had kept close enough to see where she'd gone and had pursued her into the room to torment her.

In an appeal for pity, she said, "I'm feeling ill."

Harry grinned coldly. "Too bad."

"You don't care!" she hurled back as she struggled to her feet.

He glanced up maliciously as she towered over him. "You're right!" he said in his high-pitched voice. "And since you were so anxious to come in here, you can stay here until Solon arrives!"

With that the midget darted out of the dressing room and closed the door after him, slamming a bolt into position on the

11

outside. She ran to the door and tried it, but he'd locked her in.

Pounding on the door, she begged, "Please don't shut me up in here! I won't try to escape! I promise!"

There was no reply from the other side of the door. Tears brimmed in her eyes as she turned and went back to sit in the plain chair and lean her elbows on the make-up shelf as she rested her head in her hands. In her misery she could only wonder how much more she could endure, how much longer this torment would go on! It seemed so long ago that it had all begun and yet it was no more than a few months. Yet in those months she felt she had lived a lifetime. Whenever she went over it in her mind she knew the starting point had been when she'd returned to the family estate after being out to the West Coast for a championship swimming meet.

She'd come back to Hartford on an evening flight. She'd won first place in the national swimming contest and her photo in an attractive bikini along with an account of her athletic prowess were being featured in papers and on the television all across the nation. In a minor way she was a celebrity.

She was anxious to return home because

she disliked being parted from her younger sister, Emily. There were just the two of them, now. Their mother had died shortly after Emily's birth; three years ago their father had died, leaving Gale and Emily alone in the family mansion in West Hartford. The executor of the estate, an older cousin named James Garvis, had come to live with them. He was a bachelor, a lawyer, well qualified to look after their complicated business affairs.

Their parents' death had left Gale and Emily very wealthy, as well as very lonely. James Garvis could not fill the place their devoted father had held in their lives, though he tried to do all he could for them. When Gale stepped off the jet from Los Angeles it was the slim, reserved James Garvis who came forward from the waiting crowd to greet her.

His thin, rather haggard face revealed a smile as he took her in his arms and kissed her on the cheek. He was dark with a small mustache. "I'm glad you're back, Gale," he said.

She smiled at him. "I'm always itching to return home as soon as a meet is finished," she said. "Where is Emily?"

He frowned slightly. "She decided not to come. To be frank, that Rufe character is hanging around again and she didn't want to leave him."

"Rufe?" she asked, surprised. "I thought he'd moved on to New York." Rufe was a boy Emily had known at college. Lately he turned hippie and was now devoting himself to experiments in drugs and spiritualism. Gale hadn't been too fond of the lanky youth but she had an idea Emily might be in love with him.

As they walked toward the luggage ramp in the busy airport, James went on disapprovingly, "Rufe turned up the day after you left. He's been at the house ever since — just as weird as ever. This time he's on a Ouija board kick."

"A Ouija board kick?"

James nodded with a hint of disgust. "You know, those wooden boards with letters printed on them. You have a pointer which moves under your hand to rest on the letters and spell out messages. Supposed to be a way of talking with the spirit world."

"I've heard of them," Gale said. "But I can't imagine Emily believing in anything like that."

"She seems to go along with it," their cousin worried. "I'll tell you more about it in the car after I get your bags."

She waited while he went to the revolving

14

rack to pick out her luggage. She had reservations about Rufe and his influence on her sister. Rufe had stayed around Hartford a few months and Emily had seen a lot of him. Gale hadn't gotten along too well with him, thinking his long brown hair untidy and his fringed leather outfits pretentious. But for Emily's sake she'd been pleasant with him, although she'd begun to suspect that he used marijuana.

A few weeks ago he'd announced he was moving on to New York City. Gale had been relieved at the thought he wouldn't be with Emily while she was away. Now it seemed he had changed his mind and returned.

James Garvis joined her with her bags in hand and they went out to his car. As he eased it out of the parking lot, he fretted about Rufe. "I'm sure he's taking drugs," he said, "and I'm worried about Emily. There's every reason to fear he'll try to involve her. I can see him as a pusher."

It was something she'd worried about herself. She turned to the thin dark man at the wheel of the black limousine with a troubled expression. "If it's true, we should try to somehow get rid of him."

James nodded. "I've been waiting for you to get back. Uneasily, I might add. I was going to phone you but I thought it might upset you and spoil your chances of winning the meet. By the way, congratulations."

"Thanks," she said without any interest, all her thoughts on the problem of Rufe now.

"You know how Emily resents me," the man at the wheel went on bitterly. "She has the idea I'm trying to insinuate myself in your father's place and that isn't so."

"She's never really gotten over Dad's death. You mustn't hold it against her."

"I understand," he said. "But it still makes it difficult. It's hard for me to discipline her. She misinterprets my every move."

"Have you tried to reason with her about Rufe?"

"When I've had the opportunity," he said, as they left a busy main street to turn into a quieter side one. "But Rufe is almost always around. I've been putting off any real show-down until you came home. I feel with you to back me up I can manage Emily better."

"I hope so," Gale worried. "Remember she and I don't always see things the same way either."

"You can still reach her better than I," James assured her.

Gale stared out into the gathering dusk, a frown on her pert face. "I only hope so," she said.

"He's gotten her on this spiritualism kick,"

16

her cousin grumbled.

"Don't you think that's more likely to be just a kind of game?" Gale asked. "I'm sure Emily doesn't *believe* in Ouija boards."

Her cousin gave her a warning glance. "Don't be too sure. He's been staying at the house for a week. And they've had that board out every night."

She sat back against the seat with a sigh as she stared at the familiar vista of private houses lining the street of the wealthy neighborhood. "It looks as if we'll really have to do something," she said.

As they neared the driveway to her home she tried to plan how she'd approach Emily. She would need to be discreet. Emily liked to be in the forefront of every new movement. She'd been a political activist at college and that was how she'd won Rufe's admiration. Just lately she'd been working for the Women's Lib cause. Usually Gale tried to ignore her sister's passing enthusiasms, but it looked as if Rufe might come under a different category.

James turned the car into the driveway with its rows of elms on either side and within a moment they were in front of the stately brick mansion that had been built by her grandfather.

James said, "I'll depend on you to have a

serious talk with her as soon as you can."

"I will," she'd promised.

And the opportunity came almost at once. Gale went directly to her bedroom on the second floor and from the window saw Rufe strolling across the rear lawn in the dusk. He was walking toward a greenhouse where flowers and early vegetables were grown. She decided that Emily must be somewhere in the house and alone. She left her room and went down the hall to Emily's bedroom.

The door was partly ajar and she could see that the lamp on the dresser was lighted. Emily was seated in a tall-backed chair before it, studying something. Gale opened the door and went in; Emily did not seem aware of her presence. Her gaze was fixed on a small framed photo she was holding. Gale went closer to her and to her surprise saw that it was a likeness of their dead father Emily was staring at so intently.

"Emily!" she said.

Her sister started and looked up at her. "Oh, it's you, back," she said. "I knew James was going for you but I didn't hear you arrive."

Gale frowned slightly. "You didn't even seem to hear me coming into this room."

Emily's eyes behind her large-lensed

glasses were placid. "That's because I was meditating."

"Meditating?"

"Yes. Every night before Rufe and I sit down at the Ouija board I spend a half-hour meditating. I concentrate on father. It's easier with his photo before me. Then when I try to contact him with the Ouija board I'm more in tune with him."

Gale stared at her sister in distress. "Emily, that's not healthy!"

Emily stood up, the portrait still in her hand. "Why not?"

"This brooding over Dad's photo. I know if he were alive he wouldn't approve of it!"

Emily looked at her calmly. "I happen to know he does approve. He told me so the other night."

Gale was shocked. "You can't mean that! You don't really believe that father talked to you! Father is dead!"

"To you perhaps," Emily said with a smile of triumph, "but not to me. Rufe has shown me how to reach him with the Ouija board!"

"Rufe!" Gale said scornfully.

"You needn't say his name that way."

"That *jerk!*"

"Rufe knows what he's doing," Emily maintained.

"I'll agree with you there," Gale warned

her sister. "He knows exactly what he's doing. That's why he's trying to make you believe all this madness. To get you under his influence."

Emily put the photo of their father on the dresser and walked a few steps away from her. Standing with her back partly to Gale, she said, "If you have any ideas of turning me against Rufe you'd better save them. I love him and I believe in him."

Gale hesitated, then said, "I won't argue about your love for each other. But I will question this spiritualism thing. He can't reach father's spirit and have him talk to you and you should know that!"

"I have talked with Dad since you've been away," Emily said stiffly. "You don't understand!"

"How did Dad talk to you?" she demanded.

Emily turned to her, and now the eyes behind the large glasses were full of excitement. "Through the Ouija board. He even predicted you would win the swimming meet. And you did!"

Gale sighed. "*Everyone* predicted that. I was named the favorite to win long before the affair began."

"You just don't believe in anything!" Emily declared.

"I believe that Dad loved us dearly and if he had any means of reaching us and wanted to do it he'd find other means than a Ouija board and a freak like Rufe!"

"Am I a freak, Gale?"

She wheeled around indignantly to see Rufe standing in the doorway. "Yes, I'm afraid so," she said.

"Why?" the tall, long-haired youth asked with quiet patience.

"Because of this nonsense you've been feeding Emily about the Ouija board and talking to the spirit world. It's much too corny a line for you. I'd given you credit for something newer and more convincing."

He lounged into the room, looking scornful. "Everything is corny when people don't understand. Why don't you give me a chance to prove what I've learned about the Ouija board?"

Emily turned to her pleadingly. "Yes, why don't you, Gale? Must you always be stubborn?"

She hesitated. Unwilling to alienate Emily further, she wanted desperately to prove that Rufe was either misguided or a charlatan. The question was, how best to do it? The quickest way might be to sit through one of his demonstrations and show Emily how silly the whole business was.

She said, "Are you suggesting I consult the Ouija board?"

Rufe shrugged. "Your mind is probably too closed to get any results. But at least you could sit by while Emily and I try to reach your father."

Gale looked at him grimly. "Yes," she said. "I'd really enjoy doing that."

"Do you mean it?" Emily asked.

"Yes," she said.

Rufe's long, boyish face brightened. "Then come downstairs now and we'll begin the evening's séance," he suggested.

"Don't back out!" Emily said.

Gale looked from one to the other coolly. "I won't back out," she told them. "But first I'm going to have a shower and change into some other clothes. I'd also like some coffee. I'll be with you in the living room in a half-hour."

"We'll be down there waiting," Rufe promised.

Emily linked her arm through his protectively. "I'm counting on you, Gale," she said.

"I'll be there." And with that she went out, leaving them standing together.

Back in her own room, she showered and changed. She was standing before the dresser doing her hair when a knock came on her bedroom door.

She went over and opened it to find her cousin James standing there. "I was just on my way down to have some coffee," she told him.

He came into the room and in a controlled but angry tone asked, "What is this about your going to take part in a séance with those two?"

"Oh, that?" She lifted her eyebrows. "Word spreads quickly."

"*That* kind of word," he replied contemptuously. "I thought you were going to help me, not encourage them in this nonsense."

"Oh, for heaven's sake," she said through her teeth. "I *do* intend to help you. And this is how I'm going to do it. I can't disprove the business unless I'm a witness to it."

He stared at her. "So that's why you agreed."

"Of course."

James Garvis looked bleak. "I don't suppose it can do any harm. I thought at first that creep had gotten around you, just as he has Emily."

"Hardly," she said.

"Do you think they're on drugs together? Does that explain their hearing your father's voice?"

"I don't think so," she said with a sigh.

23

"So far as I know, they don't *hear* Dad. He spells out things for them."

"Oh, lord. Well, I'm going to keep out of the way. I wouldn't want to interfere with the spirits."

Gale saw him to the door and told him, "You mustn't be too bitter toward Emily. You know she's still upset about father's sudden death."

"I'll make a point to remember that," he said as he left.

A few minutes later she followed him downstairs. Going to the kitchen, she said hello to the cook, who had been with the family for years. The old woman offered her congratulations and quickly made the cup of instant coffee which Gale requested. Taking the coffee with her, Gale went on to the living room.

Entering the double doorway of the familiar room, she felt a sudden chill of uneasiness. Rufe had drawn all the drapes; the only light in the big room came from a small lamp on the table on which the Ouija board rested. Emily was already seated there in the near darkness, the glow from the single weak light casting a ghostly reflection on her young face. Rufe was standing by her. He waved to the two remaining chairs at the table and said, "Take either one."

24

Gale hesitated, still holding the coffee cup. "Is all this stage management necessary?"

Rufe eyed her calmly. "We need a dark room. Spirits prefer it."

"Come, now!" she rebuked him.

"I believe in spirits," he said stonily. "And I defer to the conditions most favorable to them."

"And Dad prefers our living room to look like the scene of a mystery drama?"

Emily frowned at her from the table. "Please, Gale! You're wasting time!"

"And destroying the mood we've tried so hard to create," Rufe said with a hint of bitterness. "Is this how you plan to cooperate?"

She sighed. "All right. So you want me to sit at the table?"

"Yes," Emily said, "sit on my right."

Gale put the half-empty cup of coffee on an end table and went over and sat down beside her sister. Rufe then sat in the chair opposite her.

Emily gave him a worried look. "I sort of feel something at this moment," she said. "Like a cold breeze circling the table."

Rufe's eyes glistened and he leaned to the younger girl eagerly. "That could be the influence. Grasp it. Close your eyes and put your hands on the planchette!"

"Yes!" Emily whispered nervously and she placed both hands lightly on the triangle of wood.

Rufe took a pad of paper and pencil and told Emily, "I'm ready. Begin as soon as you like."

Emily's eyes were closed and her face had gone strangely pale. After a hushed moment she began to moan softly. Knowing how ridiculous it was, Gale nonetheless felt cold terror grip her. Her sister had become a tortured, eerie figure as she swayed over the Ouija board in the darkened room.

"Father!" Emily whispered loudly.

"Go on!" Rufe said.

"Father! He's near!" Emily whispered again.

"This is ridiculous!" Gale protested, at the same time knowing she was thoroughly frightened.

Rufe gave her an angry glance across the table. "Shut up!"

"Father has a message!" Emily said in the same eerie whisper.

"Tell him we're ready," Rufe said, putting one hand on Emily's and picking up a pencil with the other.

"Now!" Emily moaned.

Gale watched with distaste as the pointer began to glide over the polished board. As it began to single out letters, Rufe jotted them down.

"All!" Emily whispered.

"I have it!" Rufe exulted and he passed the pad over to Gale to examine.

She took it in trembling fingers. On it she saw the letters: "J-A-M-E-S-E-V-I-L". She stared at them and passed the pad back to Rufe again.

"Did you read the message?" he asked.

"I saw a lot of letters," she said. "I can't see that they meant anything."

"Of course they do," he said, holding up the pad. "It says James and evil. James is evil. I think that should be clear enough for anyone!"

Gale shook her head. "That was too easy," she said.

"Easy!" Rufe declared indignantly. "Look at her!"

Emily had fallen back in her chair in a kind of faint. Her head was limply to one side and her face was devoid of color. She looked . . . dead.

"Emily!" Gale cried, getting to her feet. She turned to Rufe, demanding, "What have you done to her? Given her some drug?"

"Take it easy," he said. "She's in a trance, that's all. She'll come out of it."

"I don't believe it's any trance!" she retorted angrily. "You've given her some kind of drug. I'm sure of it!"

He laughed coldly. "You couldn't be more wrong."

Emily stirred in the chair and lifted her eyes to stare at them rather blankly. "Was it all right?"

"How are you?" Gale asked, kneeling by her. "You terrified me, passing out as you did!"

Her sister smiled at her wanly. "Haven't you ever seen anyone in a trance before?"

"No. And I don't accept that as an explanation for the way you were, just now," Gale said angrily. "Did he give you something?"

"Don't blame Rufe," Emily told her. "It was father."

"Father?" she echoed.

"Yes, his spirit. He took control of me and manipulated the pointer on the Ouija board," Emily assured her gravely. "You must get used to my trances," she continued. "It's the one way we can reach father."

"No!" Gale protested.

Ignoring this, Emily asked Rufe, "What did father tell us this time?"

Rufe looked grim. "It's the message we've had so many times before." He showed her the pad.

Emily gasped. "About James again!"

"Yes," Rufe said. "James is evil! That was the message. The one your father keeps trying to pound into you." He gave Gale a wilting glance. "But she doesn't want to believe it!"

Gale cried, "I don't! Anyone can see that you deliberately chose the letters. You helped guide Emily's hands on the pointer. I'm sure of it. And you made it find the letters to make up the words you wanted. You're trying to turn Emily against James so you can entirely control her."

Rufe looked gaunt. "That's a pretty serious accusation."

"I'm telling the truth," she declared.

Emily was on her feet now, her face showing a pitiful expression. "Don't talk to Rufe that way," she begged.

"I must save you," Gale told her.

"Then consider the message father gave us tonight," Emily said. "I'm sure we should be cautious about James. You talk about Rufe trying to control me, but doesn't James control us and our money?"

"James is our cousin and our good friend," Gale said impatiently. "Father trusted him to be his executor and James has worked hard for us. How can you compare him with someone like Rufe?"

"Because I *trust* Rufe," Emily said. "And I know I was in a trance tonight and the Ouija board didn't lie."

"How can you be taken in by this nonsense?" Gale demanded wearily.

"She has faith," Rufe told her.

"What has that to do with it?" she snapped.

Emily was staring at her as they stood there in the shadowed room. And her big eyes behind the glasses showed a strange light. "You should believe, Gale," she said earnestly. "For your own good. Last night father talked to me through the board and he gave me a warning for you."

"No," she protested. "Don't try to make me believe any part of it!"

"Listen!" Emily said, coming very close to her as she went on intensely, "Father had two words of warning for you, danger and madness."

Chapter Two

Gale stared at her solemn sister with incredulous eyes. "You don't expect me to believe that kind of talk?" she asked.

The long-haired Rufe spoke up. "You could do worse."

"I don't need any advice from you," Gale said waspishly.

Emily looked tragic. "You promised to give our séance a fair test."

"And I have!" she said.

Her sister shook her head. "No. You came here with your mind made up; you wouldn't believe."

"It's a waste of time trying to convince her," Rufe warned Emily as he stared sullenly at Gale.

She crimsoned. "You'll not find me as easy to deceive as Emily," she told him. "I saw your so-called séance; it was all fakery. You worked Emily up emotionally until she fainted and you directed the pointer to whatever letters you liked."

"If that's what you want to believe."

"I have no choice," Gale told him. "I

would appreciate your holding no more of these séances here."

"Gale!" her sister said defiantly. "You can't stop us! I want to go on talking to father."

"Such beliefs can only lead to madness," Gale told her younger sister. "James is upset about what you're doing and I can't blame him. He's responsible for our welfare and he knows this is bad for you."

"And bad for him!" Rufe said with a sour smile.

"Your attempts to discredit James do you no honor," Gale told him. "I think you should leave here. You've abused our hospitality."

"He can stay as long as he likes," Emily said, coming toward her in anger. "This is as much my house as yours!"

Gale studied her unhappily. "I'd hoped it wouldn't come to a quarrel!"

"It will," Emily warned her, "if you try to send Rufe away."

She sighed. "I can only hope he'll be man enough to leave on his own." And with that she turned and made her way out of the shadowed room. She felt the need of talking to someone and hoped that James would be in the study. Making her way down the hallway toward the rear of the house, she halted before the paneled study door and knocked on it gently.

James called out, "Yes?"

"It's Gale," she ventured. "Can you see me for a few minutes?"

"Of course." She heard his footsteps as he came to open the door. It swung open and he stood there waiting for her to enter.

"I'm sorry to interrupt you," she said as she came in, "but I've just had a nasty experience."

He looked grim as he closed the door. As he waved her to a chair he said, "I can imagine."

"I went to the séance as I'd decided to."

"And?"

She shook her head. "What can I say? It didn't turn out well."

Her cousin told her, "That doesn't surprise me."

"It's — it's obscene," Gale faltered. "It would be bad enough if my father wasn't being dragged into it! I can't imagine this happening to Emily. Ordinarily she's a very intelligent girl."

James shrugged. "Some of the most intelligent people are taken in by fake spiritualism."

"And that is what this is, don't you agree?"

He looked startled. "Of course. What

would make you believe otherwise? Surely he hasn't shaken your beliefs as well as Emily's?"

"No," she said. "But it was very . . . eerie. I don't want to attend another session of the sort. Emily actually collapsed. It wasn't pleasant."

"Did she get any messages from your father?"

She nodded. "One. I broke the party up after that. I was too incensed."

"What was the message?"

She hesitated. "It wasn't important."

"I'd still like to hear what it was," he insisted.

Gale was blushing. "It seemed like a weird collection of letters to me. But Rufe translated it as 'James is evil.' I had hoped not to bother you about it. It's too silly."

James looked bothered but he spoke calmly enough. "That would be Rufe up to his usual tricks. He's making attempt after attempt to discredit me in Emily's eyes."

"It won't do him any good now that I'm here," Gale promised. "And I asked him to leave."

James brightened. "Good. What was his answer?"

"Nothing," she said. "But poor Emily was awfully upset. She insisted he could stay as long as she wanted him to."

"I was afraid of something like that."

"We'll have to wait and see," she reasoned. "If I make it unpleasant enough for him and he sees he has nothing to gain, he may decide to move on."

"I hope so," James Garvis said. "But don't depend on it. He's playing for large stakes. And Emily can keep him here as long as she likes. You can complain but you can't stop her, just as she couldn't prevent you from having a house guest of your choice."

"I hope I'd not drag in anyone like Rufe," she said bitterly.

James smiled. "We both know you wouldn't. But the thing is to pound some sort of sense into Emily's head. I haven't any idea what we can do about it."

"In time she'll catch on," was her prediction. "My being here should help."

"I'd like to think so," James Garvis said. "But as long as Rufe invokes the name of your father in those séances he'll retain his hold on Emily. Not to mention that he may be giving her some kind of dope."

Gale's eyes widened. "If there's any risk of that, shouldn't we call in the police?"

"I'd prefer to avoid any nasty scandal if possible," he said. "I did promise your father to protect you two as best I could."

"And you've done well."

James looked forlorn. "I can't agree when I consider that Rufe has come in here and practically taken over. But I'll find some way to handle him. Or you and I, together, will."

Her face shadowed. "This idea of having father spell out messages on the Ouija board is shocking. I can understand why Rufe's able to impress Emily so easily. For a moment tonight in that darkened room I was really frightened. I had to fight to make myself realize that it couldn't be father guiding that pointer."

James eyed her worriedly. "Superstition lingers in all of us. That is what Rufe is up to now — exploiting Emily's childlike wish to believe in mysteries."

"Where does he come from?" she asked.

"He won't tell and nobody else seems to know," James said.

"He's well educated; I gather that he comes from a good middle-class home," she said.

"He's thrown all that down the drain," James said bitterly. "And if he keeps control of Emily he'll have her a vagabond hippie like himself."

"Not if we can help it."

"And I think we can," he said quietly.

"It's so good to have you to depend on,"

she said. "I couldn't face this if I were here alone with Emily." She leaned close to him and kissed him on the cheek.

James looked gratified. "You're the sound one, Gale. If it weren't for you I'd appeal to the bank to be relieved of this job. But knowing you appreciate my problems makes it worth carrying on."

"I do appreciate them," she assured him. "And I'm terribly grateful." She moved to the hall door. "I must go up to bed. But I had to tell you first."

"You did right," James assured her. "We must keep in close communication with each other." And he opened the door for her.

She said goodnight and went quickly up the stairs to her own room. As far as she knew Emily and Rufe remained in the living room. She was still on edge from the eerie experience at the séance table. And again she began wondering about Rufe and who he really was. When Emily had first brought him to the house she'd pretended that she knew all about him and his family background, but slowly it became apparent that she really knew nothing about him, not even his last name. Emily accepted his anonymity as legitimate protest. But Gale worried that he chose to be virtually nameless to conceal a criminal background. She knew that he was living on the thin edge and was ready to take Emily along with him. What wonderful insurance to have a girl with a few million as his willing slave! And that was what he was making Emily.

She went on worrying as she undressed and slipped into her nightgown. Drugs. At this stage she couldn't tell whether Emily might be taking anything or not. There was no doubt in Gale's mind that Rufe was familiar with drugs and perhaps an addict of some type. It was frightening, knowing the lengths addicts would go to for money to support their habits. She slid between the sheets with this new worry clouding her thoughts. Her homecoming had been anything but triumphant. Her athletic prowess was a secondary consideration at this point. Emily had ruined everything.

When Gale finally fell asleep, nightmares tormented her. She was running across the lawn in the darkness, searching frantically for her father. They'd been out walking together, but somehow she had lost him. And now she was desperate to find him again, as she was certain she was being stalked by some shadowy figure. She hesitated by one of the hedges. "Dad!" she called out in a terror-stricken voice.

There was no reply and she was so frozen with fear that she couldn't move. A distance away in the shadows she saw the dread form of her pursuer hovering warily. And she knew that it could mean a violent death for her.

All at once there was a rustle in the trees beyond the hedge and the familiar figure of her father took shape. He came toward her, smiling confidently. Her fear drained from her and she ran toward him.

Then, as they were just a few feet apart, she remembered. Her father was dead! This was a ghost she'd been about to greet. A phantom from the other side of the grave!

"No!" she protested aloud as she hesitated in going farther.

And it seemed that her father at once knew she'd seen him as a ghost. The smile left his face and was replaced by a look of concern. And very slowly his figure vanished into a gray mist.

Horrified, she realized that she was truly alone. She turned and saw that her pursuer had taken advantage of her preoccupation with her father's ghost and had slyly crept up on her. He was within reach of her. He quickly grasped her by the arm and drew her to him. She looked up through the shadows and saw Rufe, his eyes bulging with hatred. He took her throat in his strong hands and began to choke the life from her.

She twisted restlessly against the pillows, whimpering as the nightmare went on, fighting to escape it. Finally she sat up, staring around her into the darkness.

The nightmare had been so vivid that she couldn't shake it off. The ghost of her father was etched in her mind. *Could* it be that his spirit was seeking a way to reach out to her? Had he attempted to warn her by invading her nightmare? Had he also been frustrated and angered by what was going on at the Ouija board?

Or could Rufe and Emily be on the right path? Were they really getting messages from her dead father? She refused to believe this, just as she refused to accept that her father's spirit would haunt the house. She'd had all these fancies because of Rufe's tall stories. She must close her mind to spirits and the like and concentrate on making Emily come around to the same point of view.

She lay awake a long while thinking about this before her eyelids closed. When she awoke again it was nearly nine o'clock and time to get up. Although she had no particular plan of action yet, she hoped to chat with Emily at the breakfast table. But Emily ruined this idea by not appearing. Gale sat alone at the big table feeling desolate.

It wasn't an especially fine day. A kind of mist was coming down and the clouds were gray. She would have preferred rain. After breakfast she became restless and decided to walk as far as the greenhouse. So she put on her raincoat and kerchief and started out.

The day was as dark and grim as her thoughts were. She made her way through the short wet grass without glancing around her. Reaching the greenhouse she opened the door and went inside. It was a long building with two aisles, and along the aisles were various containers of growing flowers, plants and vegetables. In some areas the green plants were higher than her head.

She slowly made her way down the first aisle, recalling that this had been one of her father's hobbies, growing exotic flowers in the greenhouse and later transplanting them outside. Reaching the end of the long glass building, she paused to study a colorful orchid-like flower with curious yellow and black blooms which showed what reminded her of a skull pattern.

She was staring at the tiny yellow and black skull heads when she heard a footstep and looked up to see the lanky Rufe standing there between her and the door.

His long face showed a menacing smile. "Looking for something?"

"What?"

"You got any special reason for coming here?"

Her surprise was replaced by anger. "Why should I tell you?"

"It might be safer to."

"Is that a threat?"

He continued to stare at her. "I never bother with threats. They just serve as warnings. When the time comes I act and fast."

Gale was frightened of him but determined not to let him know it. She said, "I'm beginning to think I don't like anything about you."

He looked pleased. "That doesn't bother me a bit," he told her.

"I hardly expected it to," she said.

"We could be friends," he said.

"We've missed that chance," she replied bitterly. "Why don't you leave here and let us forget you."

"I'm about to do that."

Her eyebrows raised. "You are?"

He gave her a nasty grin. "Sure. You don't think I'd stay in a small city like this. It cramps my style."

"I can imagine."

"I mean it," he said. "Now I do like Emily but I can always take her with me or come back to her."

"Just leave my sister alone," she said tensely.

"We'll think about that," he said mockingly. "I can do it either way."

"Have some decency," she begged. "You'd soon tire of a girl like Emily. Don't break her heart!"

"She is pretty dull," Rufe admitted, and he took a step toward her. "Now you're more my type."

"Stay away from me!" Gale cried and backed up awkwardly. As she did so she stepped on a rake and it sprang upward. At once she seized it and held it in her hands as a weapon. "Now, go!"

Rufe didn't move. "Know how long it would take me to get that rake from you?" he asked lazily.

"It might take longer than you think," she warned him, crouching back against the end of the greenhouse. "And I'd manage to do you some harm in the meantime."

"Maybe and then again maybe not," Rufe said. "You came out here thinking I had some hemp stashed in this place!"

"Have you?" she demanded, all at once aware of his interest in her being there.

He was scornful. "Think I'd tell you if I did?"

"No."

"Then, why ask?"

She studied him with defiant eyes. "Because I think you have. That's why you were so worried about my being here."

His smile remained unpleasant. "I wouldn't worry that pretty little head of yours about it," he said softly.

"I want you to go and leave me," she said, holding up the rake as if to strike him.

He regarded the move insolently. "You wouldn't dare," he said. "Your little sister would never forgive you!"

"Emily will soon see through you and your tricks," she told him.

The lanky hippie gave her a sharp look. "That Ouija board business is on the level," he told her. "There's no trick to it."

"You're lying!"

"No," he said solemnly. "That's one thing you can depend on. Your father is trying to get through to you girls."

She felt that chill run up her spine again. But she fought her fear knowing that Rufe was trying to instill the same superstition in her he'd used to such effect in Emily.

"I don't frighten as easily as my sister," she warned him.

"Maybe it would be better for you if you did," Rufe told her.

As he finished saying this James Garvis came into the greenhouse at the main entrance. Apparently he sized up the situation immediately for he came striding down to them. Rufe glanced at him over his shoulder but didn't seem unduly perturbed by his sudden appearance.

James demanded, "What's going on here?"

"He's been threatening me," Gale told him. "And I'm almost sure he has some of the weed hidden in here!"

"Marijuana," James said angrily. "I've suspected you were mixed up in drugs from the start!"

Rufe gave him an overbearing glance. "That could take some proving," he warned him.

"I'll chance that," James declared. "If you're not away from here in an hour I'm calling the police."

For the first time Rufe lost some of his cool. "Why should the police be interested in me?"

James said, "Suppose we find that out."

"Emily won't want me to go," Rufe warned him.

James snapped, "I'll chance that. I've given you my ultimatum. The rest is up to you."

45

Rufe turned quickly to Gale. "You may be sorry when I'm gone."

"I'll chance that," she told him.

"You don't know what you may be in for," Rufe warned her. "You know what your father's message said about you. Madness and danger. I'd think about that."

"Get out of here!" James Garvis ordered.

"Okay," Rufe said. "I'll go. But there'll be someone around here who'll be sorry about my leaving pretty soon." He turned to her again with one of his mocking smiles. "Write that down in your diary when you get time, Gale. You'll be thinking about it later." He brushed past James and made his exit from the greenhouse.

Her cousin gave a deep sigh of relief. "I think we've called his bluff. I have an idea he doesn't want any traffic with the police. And I'll bet he's got some drugs hidden out here."

She had put the rake down. "He's a strange person," she said quietly.

"He's a crackpot and a trouble-maker along with it," James said. "We can't be rid of him too soon."

Gale didn't see Rufe again. By the time she returned to the house he'd gathered up his things and left. Nor was Emily anywhere in sight — had she run off with the hippie?

46

Gale hurried up to Emily's room. It was empty.

Now Gale began searching the house frantically. She was about to give up in despair when she thought of the attic. And while she was making her way along the narrow hallway of the attic she heard muffled sobs coming from one of the several storage rooms. When she opened the door, she discovered Emily in the murky room kneeling on the rough plank floor in front of a large framed photo study of their mother and father. It had been taken years before, only months in advance of their mother's death.

When their father was alive, this picture had hung in the hallway not far from his study door. With his passing Gale had found the likeness of her parents too depressing to have around, so she'd ordered it sent to the attic.

She bent down to the sobbing Emily. "What's the matter? What has brought you up here?"

Emily stared at her unhappily. "You don't understand," she said. "You don't know what it means to be really lonely."

"How can you be so sure?" Gale had asked quietly.

"Because you're cold. You have to be to send Rufe away as you did. You knew how much I cared for him," Emily said brokenly.

"Did he care for you?"

"Yes," Emily insisted between sobs. "Yes!"

"If that's true, he'll return," she said.

"No," Emily said disconsolately. "I'm sure he'll never come back."

"If he loves you he will."

Emily shook her head. "No. We quarreled. He wanted me to go along with him and I refused."

She knelt down by her sister and placed an arm around her. "I don't want to judge Rufe harshly," she said. "But I believe you were wise."

"Cowardly," her sister said. "I couldn't bear to think of leaving here. Especially not since I've made contact with father's spirit."

Gale frowned. "You must get that out of your head as well. It's morbid of you to come up here and worship this old picture. Neither mother nor father would want you to become obsessed by their shadows."

Emily looked at her with tragic eyes. "The trouble is you don't believe I've really talked to father. And I'm certain that I have."

"Rufe made you think so. Part of his plan to have power over you."

"There's more to it than that," Emily said in a hushed voice. "I have heard father in the house."

The chilling fear returned to her. In a voice with a slight tremor, she asked, "When have you heard father?"

"At nights. In his room. Remember how he sometimes used to pace back and forth before going to bed? I have halted outside his bedroom door around midnight and heard his heavy steps. And when I opened the door the room was empty."

Gale was shocked. "You must have imagined it!"

"No. I really heard his footsteps. I recognized them because he always had a pattern of setting one foot down heavier than the other. You could tell his footstep."

This was true, Gale knew. Her father had had a distinctive manner of walking. But she couldn't accept Emily's testimony that there was a ghost in the house. This had to be a hallucination.

She said, "I'm sure that Rufe must have been with you when you heard those ghostly footsteps. No doubt he alerted you to them."

Emily startled her further by saying, "No. I was alone when I heard it."

"Did you hear these ghostly footsteps at any other time?"

"Yes."

"When?"

"On the front stairway," Emily said, a strange far-off expression on her face. "Rufe and I both heard him on the front stairs several times."

Gale swallowed hard. "I don't know what to say. I hate to hear you going on this way." She eyed her sister sharply. "Have you and Rufe been taking any kind of drugs?"

Emily shook her head. "Not lately. When we first met we smoked some marijuana together. And once he gave me tablets that made me see things in weird colors and put everything out of focus. I was frightened and wouldn't take any more of them."

"I see," she said. "So you were in a clear state of mind when you heard these manifestations?"

"Yes."

"I'd like to be more understanding," she sighed. "But I can only tell you I'll believe you when I am exposed to some of those happenings myself."

Emily looked at her sorrowfully. "You're very skeptical."

"I can't help it."

"You can do something for me now that Rufe isn't here anymore," her sister said. "I need someone to help me with the séances."

Her eyes widened. "You're surely not going on with that sick business!"

"I must!" Emily insisted, turning to stare at the picture of their parents again. "I feel so close to father now."

"Don't ask me to encourage you in this morbidity," she protested.

"There's no one else now that you've sent Rufe away! James won't come into the room when the Ouija board is set up. Sometimes I get the feeling he's afraid of it."

"More likely he wants to make clear his complete disapproval of it just as I do," Gale said.

"Please, Gale," her sister said.

"I'll think about it." She managed to get Emily out of the stale dampness of the attic and downstairs, hoping that with Rufe gone the house would be restored to normalcy. Emily's account of hearing their father's footsteps she put down to overwrought nerves.

As evening came a drizzle turned to a downpour of rain. When they all met at the dinner table James Garvis tried to be as friendly to Emily as he could, but she ignored him most of the time. It was apparent she blamed him for Rufe leaving. When dinner ended, James mentioned having to go into Hartford for a meeting, and shortly after he left.

Gale was standing by the living room windows staring out at the teeming rain when Emily came quietly up to her. Her younger sister's face was serious as she said, "I'd like to try and contact father tonight. I feel the atmosphere is right."

She turned to her. "Must you?"

"Yes."

"Very well," she said in a bleak voice. "What do you want me to do?"

Emily brightened. "I'll show you."

She at once began closing the drapes of the big room and turning down the lights. Gale watched as her sister brought the table to its regular place before the divan and set the Ouija board and the pointer on it. When she had arranged a single chair by it and placed the small lamp there for a subdued lighting effect she stood back.

"I'm ready," Emily said. "I'll sit on the divan and you use the chair."

Reluctantly Gale advanced to the table with the Ouija board. "What do I do?"

"Sit down and I'll tell you," her sister said. And when they were both seated at the table Emily continued, "After I have fallen into a trance I will begin to move the pointer across the Ouija board. You must place your hand on mine and lightly follow my guidance. As I seek out letters you will note them down. And if we're able to get through to father the letters will spell out a message."

Gale gave a tiny shudder. "I don't like it at all!"

"You'll feel differently about it after we begin," Emily promised her.

"I doubt it."

"Now I'm going to attempt a trance," Emily said with a solemn glance her way. And she closed her eyes as the soft glow of the lamp was reflected on her glasses.

Gale sat there in the shadows watching her sister closely. Emily's hands were on the pointer and with her eyes closed and her body held rigid she seemed to be deeply concentrating. The color drained from her cheeks and then her mouth twitched. She moaned and swayed a little in the chair. The moaning came again, louder this time. And she began to move the pointer across the lettered board.

Gale followed instructions by lightly placing her hand on her sister's. And she was startled by the cold, clammy feel of Emily's hand. Now the pointer began to seek out various letters. As it did Gale used her free hand to jot them down. The board was moving at a feverish rate and it took all her concentration to keep up with it. Finally, with a deep sigh, Emily let go of the pointer and slumped back in her chair. She seemed to have fainted.

Gale stared down at the pad and the uneven line of letters she'd jotted there: "E-M-I-L-Y-W-I-L-L-D-I-E".

For a few seconds her mind refused to separate the words into the message. "Emily will die!" With fear choking her, she lifted her eyes from the pad to the still-unconscious Emily.

Chapter Three

Frantically Gale got to her feet and tried to revive the pale and motionless Emily. Her sister's head lolled like that of someone dead as she raised her a bit in the chair. Then to her utter relief Emily's eyelids fluttered and she opened them to stare up at her blankly.

"Are you all right?" Gale gasped.

"Yes," was Emily's weak reply.

"You frightened me terribly," she went on. "I couldn't seem to rouse you."

"I could hear you," Emily said. "But I wasn't able to move or speak."

She stared at her with startled eyes. "So you actually were in some sort of trance!"

"Of course."

"I'd never been alone with you before when you were like this. I was at my wit's end!"

"I always come out of the spells," Emily said. "I'm sure I reached father again this time. I could almost hear his voice."

She stared at her in fear and confusion. "You honestly believe that?"

"Yes. Did you get the message?"

"I copied the letters," she said tautly. And she suddenly realized that it would only frighten Emily and send her into new excesses of morbidity if she should see the message. She reached for the pad and kept it in her hand. "They didn't add up to anything. Probably because I didn't know how to go about it as Rufe did."

Emily stood up, the eyes behind her glasses showing doubt. "I can't believe that," she said. "I have the distinct impression there was a message."

"I'm sorry."

"Let me see the pad," Emily demanded as they stood there facing each other in the near darkness of the large living room.

"It's not important."

"Please!" Emily held out her hand.

"It doesn't make sense!" she protested.

"I'd prefer to be the judge of that."

She still hesitated, realizing she should have destroyed the sheet of paper before Emily came to. Now it seemed there was nothing to do but let her see it. Reluctantly she let her have the pad.

Emily took it and stared at it for a long moment, then looked up solemnly. "Why did you try to keep this from me?"

"I don't believe it! It's just one of those crazy happenings!"

"No," her sister reproved her. "I don't agree."

"You surely aren't going to take the message seriously? Because it says you're going to die you're not going to meekly await death?"

"Father merely wants to prepare me," Emily said in her sober way. "I'm not afraid."

"It's all nonsense," Gale protested though there was a tremor of fear in her voice.

Before Emily could answer, they heard footsteps on the front stairway — clear at first, the sound faded as the feet mounted the stairway to the second floor. And the sound was unmistakable. Her father's footsteps! The two girls exchanged frightened glances.

Emily said, "I told you!"

"It has to be someone else!" Gale insisted and ran down the room and out in the hallway to gaze up the empty stairway with frightened eyes.

Emily had followed her and now stood at her side. "I told you there would be no one there. It was father you heard."

Gale turned on her. "I do not believe in ghosts."

Her younger sister said quietly, "I do." And she went on up the shadowed stairway in the wake of the ghostly footsteps.

Left alone, Gale returned to the living room and opened the drapes once again and turned on the lights. She went over to the Ouija board which Emily had left sitting on the table. It looked harmless enough and yet it was creating a sinister atmosphere in the old house. Turning away from its bright polished surface she decided she'd wait up for James Garvis and tell him about the evening.

It was after midnight when she heard his key turn in the front door. She put aside the magazine she was reading and went out to meet him.

He looked surprised to see her. "You're up late."

"Yes. It's been quite a night."

"Oh?"

"I wanted to talk to you about it for a minute," she said, glancing toward the stairway where Emily had earlier vanished.

James removed his dark topcoat and hesitated. "Shall we go into the study?"

"I think so."

He led her down the hall to the study and they went inside. When he'd closed the door, he asked, "What's been going on?"

She smiled tremulously. "I allowed Emily to talk me into assisting her in a séance."

"Any normal person would try to avoid the

58

stupid business," James said with disgust.

She took a deep breath. "After tonight I must admit I'm not so sure about that."

His thin face was grim. "You begin to sound more and more like your sister."

She blushed. "I can't help it."

"Tell me what went on."

Briefly she gave him an account of the séance and the message she'd gotten from the letters. As she finished, she said, "I should have torn up the sheet with the message on it. I didn't. And so I had to let Emily see it."

"I can imagine her reaction," James said with annoyance.

"She believed it. I'm afraid it will make her worse than ever."

"You should have refused to sit down at the Ouija board with her."

"I suppose so," she worried. "And yet she's so lonely and confused I hated to do that."

"So now you have the result."

"That was bad enough," she said, meeting his eyes directly. "But right after something more frightening happened. We both heard father's footsteps on the front stairs."

James Garvis frowned. "You heard footsteps on the stairs," he said by way of correction.

A taut silence filled the somber room for a moment before Gale replied evenly, "No. I heard my father's footsteps. He had a distinctive walk. You couldn't mistake it. We went to the bottom of the stairway and we could see no one."

"So you at once ran away with the idea you'd heard a ghost," her cousin said with sarcasm. "Only your upset nerves can explain your repeating such a story. In the morning you'll feel differently about it."

"I wonder."

"You heard one of the servants. They have a way of appearing and disappearing. And your imagination filled in the rest."

Gale sighed. "I wish I could agree. But I can't. At least not yet. Also, Emily told me earlier she had heard father pacing in his room."

He walked wearily across the room and fumbled with some papers on the desk. His back partly to her, he said, "What do you expect me to say in answer to such talk? You know who started all this. That hippie character, Rufe."

"I think Emily has also been delving into spiritualism on her own."

"What if she has?" James said, turning to her angrily. "Is that any reason for you to take it up? I counted on you to be a stabilizing influence on her. You're certainly a disappointment."

"It's just that I can't explain what happened here tonight," she lamented.

"You allowed Emily to make a fool of you," he said. "I'm sorry but I have to put it to you bluntly. The best thing you can do for the moment is go to bed and forget about it all."

"I'm afraid that won't be easy."

"Easy or not, it's the answer," James assured her.

"I waited up for you because I felt I needed your advice."

He smiled bleakly. "And I've given you the best I can offer."

"I know," she said, looking down. "Please don't think me ungrateful."

His hand was on her arm. "I understand," he said. "Emily has always been a sensitive, high-strung girl and this Rufe worked on her nerves until she's almost on the point of collapse."

"She is in a very strange state."

"Perhaps I should have tried to get rid of him before you returned," the lawyer worried. "But I thought it best to have your approval. In the end he didn't offer much resistance."

"He tried to get Emily to leave with him."

"I'm not surprised."

"Thank Heavens she had the good sense to refuse."

James nodded. "Basically she's as sound as you are. Once he's been away for a little I have an idea she'll get over all this nonsense."

"I hope so." She hesitated. "But I'm still not satisfied as to what happened."

"Try not to think about it. A sound night's rest will make all the difference."

"Perhaps," she said as she moved toward the door.

He followed her. "Don't think I'm unsympathetic. And don't be afraid to bring any other problems like this to me," he told her as he opened the door for her.

"Thank you, James," she said sincerely. "And good night."

The following day was warm and sunny. Somewhat uneasily, Gale invited Emily to go for a stroll. She wanted to talk about the previous night, but didn't know how to begin. Almost in silence, they went as far as the greenhouse and back, then took chairs on the patio. Emily was wearing a broad-brimmed white sun hat and dark glasses and looked more healthy than she had in some time.

It was Emily who first introduced the subject. She said, "I don't blame you for trying to hide the message that came through on the Ouija board last night."

"I'm not even sure I got it right," Gale replied.

Her sister looked wise. "It was clear enough," she said. "Father warned me that I'm soon going to die."

"It didn't read that way. It simply said 'Emily will die', which could mean anything or nothing. Everyone dies sooner or later. It named no time."

"It will be soon."

"How can you be so sure?"

"I feel it. Something awful is going to happen here. And it will mean my death."

Gale leaned forward to her with a reproving frown. "How can you sit here in the sun on this lovely day and have such dreadful thoughts?"

"I can't help it."

"You must fight this morbid nonsense," Gale argued. "Rufe started you on it. I must say he was an unhealthy influence."

"I love Rufe," her sister said. "Please don't talk about him like that."

She sank back in her chair with a sigh. "Why did he get you so involved in spiritualism?"

"He believes in it. You saw what happened last night. The message had to come from father."

"You could easily have sought the letters out yourself even though you don't remember doing it," Gale said.

"I was in a trance. Remember?"

"It could be that your subconscious mind still controlled your actions."

"What about father's footsteps?"

Gale hesitated. "I've decided it had to be one of the servants on the stairs."

Her sister smiled scornfully. "That sounds like James' talk. But you can't deny that you recognized father's way of walking. I saw your face before you ran out to the stairs. You were terrified."

"All right," she said. "I'll admit I was upset. That the footsteps did resemble father's. But I was in an emotional state. I made a mistake."

"I don't think so," Emily said quietly.

She studied her sister with serious eyes. "Emily, you really must fight this. I can't bear to have you become a neurotic who believes in ghosts and similar spiritualistic nonsense. There are just the two of us. We need to fight this together."

"But we see this through different eyes," Emily said.

"I'm trying to help you back to a healthy

point of view," Gale said.

"I don't need it."

"That's not true!"

Emily's voice was edged with anger as she demanded, "Is there anything wrong in my wanting to contact father? You know how I've missed him since his death. His messages help me."

"Your preoccupation with the dead isn't normal," she protested. "I was shocked to find you seated before that old picture in the attic crying your heart out."

"Don't you ever feel lonesome for Mother and Dad?" her sister wanted to know.

"Of course I do, in a natural way," she said. "But I don't think I can bring them back from the dead. And what is more I know they wouldn't want it. They'd be sick if they knew how you were mooning about trying to get spirit messages."

Emily stood up. "The trouble is you don't believe. You have no faith in spiritualism."

"I'll admit it."

"Then it's no use," her sister said. "I can see now I was wrong not to have left with Rufe when he asked me. Now something dreadful is going to happen because I didn't."

"What do you mean by that?" Gale asked sharply. "Did Rufe threaten you when you quarreled?"

"Of course not!" Emily said. "Can you imagine him threatening me?"

Emily's response had been quick enough — but how could Gale know if she was telling the truth? "I'm sorry," she said, anxious to remain friendly with the younger girl. "I don't want us to quarrel."

"We won't," Emily assured her calmly. There was something strange in that almost arrogant calm which seemed to come over her every so often. "Of course you'll not assist me in any more séances." It was a statement rather than a question.

"I'd rather not."

"I don't want you to if you don't believe in it."

"I wish I could be more helpful," she said, standing there uncertainly.

"I'll find someone else."

"Who else is there here?"

"Maybe Rufe will come back." Emily sighed. "There's just one other thing. Please don't talk to James about the séance. He's very bitter about my experiments and it will only cause harm."

Gale tried to keep from feeling guilty by telling herself that last night's conversation with him had been for Emily's good. "I'm certain James is only anxious about you. He worries more than you realize."

Emily smiled bitterly. "I think Rufe had him sized up right. He claimed the only thing that really worried James was money."

"Rufe wasn't liable to be fair about James."

"Nor James about Rufe for that matter," Emily said darkly. "James made a bad mistake when he ordered Rufe away. Things would have been better and safer for us all if he'd remained here."

She stared at her sister with troubled eyes. "Why do you say that?"

"It's what I feel."

"You're not keeping anything from me?" she worried. "A threat that Rufe made or anything like that?"

"No," Emily said. "I'd rather not talk about it anymore."

In the days and nights that followed Emily kept a good deal to herself, and when she was with Gale she said little. This worried Gale and kept the atmosphere of the house tense. James Garvis also complained privately to her about Emily's odd behavior.

Frowning, he said, "Since Rufe left, she's moved about the house like some silent phantom."

"She was in love with him," Gale told their cousin. "I'm sure she feels bad about the way things have turned out."

"I have only tried to take care of her."

"I realize that, but she doesn't believe it."

James sighed. "We'll be lucky if Rufe doesn't come back and try to entice her away again. Or maybe he'll come in the night and try to rob the place. I wouldn't put it past him!"

"Do you really believe him capable of that?" she asked worriedly.

"Yes."

"You may be wrong," she said. "He's a rebel of course. But I've never considered him a criminal."

"Wait and see," was her cousin's warning.

There were no more séances. But several times Gale came upon Emily seated at a table setting out Tarot cards. It seemed the younger girl had turned to this solitary means of contacting the spirits to satisfy her needs.

And once in the night Gale heard the footsteps. She wakened from a deep sleep to hear someone moving about in the corridor outside her door. As she sat up in bed listening tensely, she heard the footsteps retreating — the familiar footsteps of her father. Silence returned to the dark mansion and she got up and went to the door and opened it. Looking up and down the corridor she saw no sign of anyone. Shaken, she returned to bed.

The climax of all this came on a bright morning in late June. She was awakened by an urgent knocking on her door. Sitting up, she called out, "Yes? Who is it?"

"James," came the reply from the other side of the door. "I must speak with you at once."

"Just a minute." She hurried out of bed, hastily donning her dressing gown and sliding into slippers before going to the door. When she opened it, she knew from his face that something was terribly wrong. "What is it?" she asked anxiously.

"Emily."

"No," she cried. "Don't tell me she's run off to join Rufe."

His thin face was grim. "I wish it were that."

Now she was on the edge of panic. "What then? Don't keep me in suspense!"

"Better brace yourself," James said. "She's been murdered!"

"No!" she whispered. She swayed forward faintly, but James' arm came comfortingly around her to steady her. "I've already called the police. They should be here any minute. I couldn't keep the truth from you any longer."

"When?"

"It must have happened in the middle of the night."

"How?" she asked in a dazed tone.

"Someone from the outside broke into the hall window near her room. That's how they got to her. She was stabbed with something. Blood all over. You wouldn't want to go in there."

"Poor Emily!" she said brokenly.

His arm still supporting her, he said, "I knew something of this sort could happen anytime. I felt Rufe would come back someday and kill her."

"Why Rufe?"

"Who else?"

"It could have been anyone!" she protested. "Were there signs of a theft?"

"I haven't made a thorough search," James said grimly. "But Emily liked to have plenty of cash in her purse. I'll bet it's gone along with most of her good jewelry."

"That means it might have been any thief."

"I don't see it that way," James told her. "I felt we were all in bad trouble from the time Emily brought that hippie here. Now we're reaping the full rewards."

"But you shouldn't blame him unless you're sure," she protested. "It's up to the police to investigate and find out who did it."

"They still need the facts to begin their investigation."

"As long as you're not prejudiced in offering them," she told him. "We don't want the police blaming the wrong person."

His thin face was reproachful. "Are you suggesting that I mightn't be fair?"

"I'm thinking of your personal dislike for Rufe."

"I'll try to control that," he promised.

"Please do," she said. And then with an expression of fear on her pretty face, she reminded him, "You'll remember the Ouija board predicted Emily's death."

"That has nothing to do with it," he said scornfully.

"Don't be too sure! Perhaps it was my father who gave her the message in an attempt to warn her!"

"Don't you begin with that spiritualism nonsense," James protested. "I couldn't stand it."

Their conversation was brought to an end by the arrival of the police. James went downstairs to greet them while she sat weakly for a few moments trying to collect her thoughts and fight her tendency to become hysterical. She still didn't really believe that Emily had been murdered. That at this moment her sister was stretched out on her bed a bloodied corpse!

She heard James come upstairs with the police. The rumble of voices droned on as they moved down the hallway. It was too much! Like a sleepwalker, she got up and went out into the corridor. Slowly she made her way down the hall to the open door of Emily's room. Several of the servants were gathered out there and when they saw her they respectfully moved aside.

Gale advanced to the doorway and saw the grave circle of men around the bed. James was describing his discovery of the body. And as one of the men moved to the foot of the bed she had a momentary glimpse of Emily's motionless body and saw the blood-stained bedclothes. She gasped; the men turned and gazed at her with some consternation. Then the cloak of velvety blackness descended on her and she reached for the door frame to save herself as she sank unconscious to the floor.

Her next moment of awareness came with her in bed in a room she'd never seen before — a small room with pale green walls and an antiseptic smell. It seemed to be night, for a small shaded lamp on the wall above her head was on. The table at her bedside was painted white and bare of any ornament. Then the door from the corridor opened and a uniformed nurse entered.

The nurse came to her with a friendly

smile. "You're awake! Wonderful!"

"Where am I?"

"In the hospital," the nurse said. "Don't you remember being brought in here?"

She stared at the girl with dull eyes. "No. When?"

"Several days ago."

"I don't remember."

"You wouldn't," the nurse said. "You weren't yourself. We had to give you powerful sedation. But I can see now that you're better."

She closed her eyes for a moment in an effort to think. And then that terrible quarterhour before her collapse returned to her. She opened her eyes to look up at the nurse in anguish. "Emily!"

"I know," the nurse said gently. "You must try not to think about that."

Alarm glistened in her eyes. "Where is my cousin? Where is James?"

"We can call him and tell him you're better," the nurse said. "He's been here a number of times but you were either sleeping or didn't know him."

"What time is it?"

"Nine in the evening," the nurse said.

"I want to talk to James!" Her voice rose unreasonably.

"I'll see that he's phoned at once," the

nurse promised her. "Now I think I should get Dr. Wasson to come and have a look at you. He's somewhere on this floor."

"James!" she repeated weakly and closed her eyes again.

She couldn't believe she'd become this weak and ill in such a short time. But the mere effort of saying a few words seemed to drain her small strength. She lay there with closed eyes until she heard the door of her room open and footsteps coming to her bedside. Then she looked up and had her first glimpse of the pleasant-faced young doctor.

He was dressed in a neat gray suit and had a striped crimson shirt and matching crimson tie. She was surprised that these unimportant details should catch her attention. He smiled at her and said, "I'm glad you're better."

"Am I?" she asked faintly.

"I can promise you that," he said. "When they brought you here you were pretty upset. Fortunately the shock has done you no permanent damage."

"I'm too weak to move. Why?"

"Reaction to shock and then you've been heavily sedated," he said. "Just now I'd like to get some warm liquid into you. Have any favorite soup?"

"I'm not hungry."

"You don't need to be. We had some excellent beef bouillon in the cafeteria at dinner. How about that?"

"If I must take something."

"You must."

"What about James Garvis, my cousin?"

"The nurse is placing a call to him," Dr. Wasson said. "He'll likely be here shortly. And if you want to be alert when he comes, better try to get something in your stomach."

The nurse returned with the bouillon, and word that James Garvis had been reached and would be there to talk with her shortly. When Gale finished the bouillon she sat back against the pillows which had been propped up for her.

"I must look a sight," she sighed.

The nurse smiled. "That means you are coming around quickly. I never worry once a patient begins to be concerned about her appearance."

"Are any of my personal things here?" she asked. "My handbag or an overnight case?"

"Yes," the nurse said, going to the room's single closet. "Your handbag and a case are both here. I'll bring them to you."

When the nurse set the things on the bed, Gale discovered that the housekeeper had packed a few personal items for her along with some make-up which had been on her dresser. The nurse brought her a mirror and held it for her while she attempted to improve her pale appearance a little.

By the time the familiar, thin figure of James Garvis appeared in the doorway she was somewhat more herself. His narrow features were lined with strain and weariness as he came to her bedside and touched his lips to her forehead.

"I'm so glad you're better," he murmured.

"It was stupid of me to collapse as I did," she said.

"Not at all."

"I remember so little of what happened."

"Probably nature's way of making the sad business bearable for you."

"Perhaps," she said with a sigh. "I still can't believe it."

"I know," he said.

"Have they any idea yet who did it?"

James nodded slowly. "They're of the opinion it had to be Rufe. They believe he bolstered his courage with some sort of drug and came back to the house to rob it and take Emily with him. She refused to agree to his plan and in his crazy drugged state he killed her. We're lucky he didn't try to finish the rest of us off as well."

"So that's what they think," she said dully. The report wasn't unexpected but she found it unconvincing. And she began to wonder if the truth might only be discovered by reaching out to Emily in that other world. Would the Ouija board with which Emily was so familiar offer a means?

Chapter Four

She was discharged from the hospital a week after she entered it and James Garvis drove her silently back to the house. It was the beginning of a period of nerves and tension for her. Everything about the place reminded her of Emily; she despaired of ever living a normal life there again.

The police came back several times to question her. They still hadn't located Rufe — not that she felt Rufe was the killer. She had never believed that. In her opinion Emily had been the victim of some transient who'd entered the house to rob it.

Cousin James seemed to become more withdrawn after the tragedy. She knew that he blamed himself for not having protected them better. She considered it wrong for him to feel guilty, but she also thought he had been too quick to accuse Rufe. So her feelings toward this older cousin who was her guardian were strangely mixed.

Worst of all, she was continuing to suffer from brief mental blackouts. Once she had been seated in her room and awoke later to discover that she was strolling in the garden. Another time she'd been downtown shopping and the period between the time she was in the shoe department of one store and the dress section of another was lost to her. She went home in a panic.

And there were the footsteps. Several times in the night she'd wakened to hear her father's footsteps. More than once she'd sat down with the Ouija board, caressing the smooth wood surface of the pointer and debating whether she should try to contact the spirits or not. But she lacked the courage to attempt entering in a trance as Emily had. And there was no one at the house to assist her, other than James or one of the servants. She saw no prospect of success with them.

When July came with its blistering heat she moped about the big silent house more unhappy than ever. It was dusk one evening when she was seated on the marble bench in the rose garden that James came out to stand before her.

Studying her with concerned eyes, he said, "You're miserable here, aren't you?"

She looked up at his thin presence there in the fading light. "Yes," she admitted.

"I have seen it too clearly since you've returned from the hospital," he said. "You can't get over Emily's murder."

"I'm still stunned by it."

"I know," he said. "And that's why I'm positive you must get away from here if you're going to save your health."

Her eyebrows raised. "Get away?"

"Yes. I've already made a reservation for you. I hope you won't resent my having booked you a holiday."

"I'm surprised more than resentful," she said. "A holiday? Where?"

"In Maine. At a summer hotel in Kennebunkport. I selected it because I know the place myself. It has a beautiful location and good food. I've taken a two-week reservation for you. And I'd say you should leave at once."

"I don't know," she hesitated.

"You'll be away from here. No one will know you. Emily's murder got a lot of local coverage but there was little national newspaper publicity concerning it."

"I do feel that people stare at me and whisper here," she admitted.

"Get away from here," James pleaded. "Give yourself a chance. Two weeks by the ocean will do wonders for you."

She smiled ruefully. "What about you? Why don't you come along?"

"I can't," he said. "Too many details to take care of here. It's too late to help Emily," he went on sadly, "but I can do my best for you. Promise me you'll go to Maine."

"How will I get there?"

"It's only a short drive. About three hours."

"On a busy highway," she pointed out. "I don't like to trust myself on drives with my blackouts."

"I'd forgotten about them for a moment," he said. "I'll drive you up myself and stay for dinner. That will give you time to get settled."

"I'd appreciate that," she said. "Do you think I can manage on my own in a hotel? I never know when those blank spells will strike me."

"Just make sure you never swim alone or do any driving," James said. "I'll come back for you when you're ready to return home. The change and fresh sea air can't help but do you good."

And so, despite her misgivings, Gale consented to try the seaside resort. The big white hotel sat majestically on a hill overlooking the ocean. It was at the end of a long, straight road through the small Maine town, and had pleasant lawns and gardens. It was well filled with tourists from as far away as Florida, and Gale at once took to the place.

James kept his word and remained for dinner with her. They had cocktails beside the huge swimming pool built high on rocks so that it formed a back patio to the big hotel. Tables were set out there under bright awnings and from inside there came the music of an orchestra playing in the lounge.

James, immaculate in a Palm Beach suit, smiled at her across their table. "Well, how do you like it?"

"Fine as long as you're here for company," she said. "I don't know what I'll do when I'm alone."

"You needn't worry with all this crowd here," he said. "You're bound to make friends."

"I don't find it as easy as I used to," she said. And she studied the pool with a sigh. "I suppose I can tell the guard my problem. Then I can swim here knowing he'll keep an eye on me."

"Do that," James urged her. "You must be in bad shape. You've not been in the water since your stay in the hospital. You should get back to it."

"I mean to," she said.

"That is the only answer," he told her. "You must face up to life again. There's no reason why your world should end with Emily's death. Try to keep that in mind."

"I will," she said listlessly. "Shall we eat now, or do you want another drink?"

It was at dinner that she first saw the handsome young couple who were destined to become her close friends. She and James had a table for two near the entrance of the hotel dining room and the majority of the other guests of the hotel had to pass them on the way in.

She happened to lift her eyes when a striking blonde in a chic green dress and a tall, slightly older man with receding brown hair and tanned, even features went by on their way to the other end of the dining room.

James noted her reaction to them and with wry amusement said, "I don't blame you for staring at those two. They're fine-looking people."

She blushed. "Was I staring at them?"

"It was obvious only to me," he said. "They get a nice class of people here. A couple like that are the sort to cultivate. Don't get yourself tied up with the elderly ones. They'll give you no peace. It's something like shipboard. The right friends can make your holiday and the wrong ones can ruin it."

"Just now I feel strictly like keeping to myself," she said. "I'll read and swim and just sit in the sun."

"Do all those things," James encouraged her as the waiter brought them their coffee.

It was around eight when James left. She walked through the busy lobby and out to the car with him. The drive back to Hartford would take until almost midnight so she knew she couldn't expect him to stay on any longer. Yet she was terrified at the prospect of being forced to carry on by herself in the crowded hotel.

As they stood by the car she confessed to him, "It's crazy! I find myself afraid of people! I never was like that before!"

"You had a severe shock," he said with understanding. "This is part of it. Give yourself time and you'll be your old self again. Consider this holiday as part of the therapy."

She gave him a troubled look. "If I feel I can't make it, I'll call you and you can come back for me."

He smiled sadly. "Yes, I'll do that. But I hope you won't ask me."

"I'll try not to," she said. "It's just to know I have some way of retreat if I need it."

"Try to enjoy yourself here," he urged her. "The best thing I can think of happening to you is to have you meet some nice young man and fall in love."

Her face shadowed. "Don't talk about such things."

"Why not? It's what you need. It could do wonders for you. Surely a place like this has a few eligible young men as guests."

"I tell you I'm not interested," she said.

"Think it over," James told her.

And with that startling advice he said goodbye and drove out of the semi-circular driveway of the hotel. She stood by the lower gate watching after him as he headed the car down the road to the village, giving a final wave as he turned the corner and went out of sight.

She stood there for a forlorn moment and then began slowly walking up the sidewalk to the front verandah and entrance to the hotel. It had an impressive verandah supported by huge white pillars of rounded wood. A few guests were gathered there chatting as the blue dusk settled on the warm summer night.

Gale was starting across the verandah when a woman hurried out of the hotel entrance and collided with her. The young woman's handbag fell and burst open, spilling its contents.

"I'm terribly sorry," Gale exclaimed.

"No. My fault. I was walking too fast, and not looking," the woman said as she bent down to retrieve the contents of her bag.

Gale also knelt to help her. Like all feminine handbags it had been madly over-stuffed with a myriad of items. She busily collected what she could and handed them to the woman.

"Thank you," the woman said, rising and arranging the things in her bag again. "I didn't lose anything but my dignity and I have so little of that it doesn't matter."

Gale smiled. "It's good of you to take it so well."

The woman was young, blonde and strikingly beautiful. She returned Gale's smile saying, "I can't imagine why I rushed out here as I did. I wasn't going anywhere especially."

Gale couldn't help staring at her. "I remember you," she said. "I saw you as you came into the dining room with your husband."

The woman stared at her in return. "Of course!" she exclaimed. "You were at the table by the door with that intelligent-looking dark-haired man. Your husband, I suppose?"

She shook her head. "No. My cousin. He left a few minutes ago. I'm here on my own."

"Then let me introduce myself," the young woman said. "I'm Mavis Pelham. My husband is probably downstairs in the lounge waiting for me. You must come and meet him."

She hesitated. "I don't want to intrude."

"We adore company," Mavis said. "Our bumping into each other may not have been such a tragedy after all. It's given us a chance to meet."

"I noticed you and your husband," she confessed. "I thought you were perhaps the best-looking couple to enter the dining room."

"Bless you!" Mavis Pelham said. "Don't tell my husband that. He used to be a photographer's model before he joined my father's firm in the stock market and really made it big. He's conceited enough as it is." Mavis linked an arm in hers and chattered on pleasantly as they made their way along a somewhat dark corridor to the lounge.

The orchestra was playing there and quite a few couples were seated at the tables in the wood-paneled Submarine Room.

"There he is," Mavis said, indicating a table behind the bar where her husband was sitting alone. They went across the room and he stood up as they joined him.

"Jack, I want you to meet someone special, Gale Garvis," she said. "Gale, this is my handsome Jack."

Jack, standing very erect and taller than she'd realized, gave her a warm smile. "Happy to meet you, Gale. Please sit on my right. With Mavis on my left I'll be flanked by beauty on both sides."

"A good job you added that," Mavis said in bantering fashion as they all were seated.

They talked for a few minutes and Gale felt that she had been lucky to have collided with Mavis. They seemed to know most of the guests at the hotel and talked as if they'd been coming there for quite a few seasons.

Mavis explained, "My parents brought me here first when I was a youngster. So of course when Jack and I married I wanted to introduce him to the place."

Jack smiled wryly. "She's gotten me accustomed to all kinds of expensive tastes."

The pretty blonde reached over and patted her husband's hand. "You're so right for them, darling."

Feeling nervous, Gale said, "I'm looking forward to doing some swimming."

"You like swimming?" Mavis asked.

"Yes. I've done a lot of it," she said.

Jack Pelham was now staring at her with new interest. The handsome man said, "Gale Garvis! Of course I should have recognized you when we first met. I've seen your picture in the papers and watched you on television. You're the swimming champion."

She blushed. "My secret is out."

"How wonderful!" Mavis exclaimed, and turned to her husband. "Isn't she wonderful?"

Jack was looking at Gale with an admiring expression. "You'll get no argument on that from me."

"Now you both must dance," Mavis urged them. "I see my golf partners for the morning over there and I want to talk to them. You two can keep out of mischief by going on the floor."

Within moments Gale found herself in Jack's arms dancing to the romantic music of the hotel orchestra.

Gale was thankful for the shadowed atmosphere of the small dance floor. Jack Pelham was holding her tightly and she felt her cheeks burning. She began to think the handsome man was a flirt.

She said, "I feel guilty. I'm spoiling the evening for you and your wife."

"Nonsense," he said, as if he meant it.

"There's that old adage about three being a crowd. It makes a lot of sense. Especially when you two are on vacation."

He offered her a mocking smile. "You're suggesting that you might spoil our recapturing our romantic honeymoon mood? That's hardly likely after all these years. We like company."

"You'd be polite about it anyway," she worried.

"I'm not all that considerate by nature," he assured her. "See, Mavis is still at the table with her golf pals. It's an obsession with her and I'd prefer to swim. I spend most of my time at the pool with a spot of tennis wedged in now and then."

"I like the water too."

"You must or you wouldn't have won yourself all those silver cups," he said.

"I was lucky most of the time."

"You're modest and pretty," the handsome man said. "A remarkable combination."

She felt compelled to say, "I think Mavis is particularly attractive."

"She is," he agreed. "But never modest. I can promise you that."

She managed a small smile. "Husbands rarely appreciate their wives' good qualities."

"Consider me an exception," he said. "But I'm still aware of beauty in other women. And I demand the privilege of paying tribute to it when I see it."

"You'll wind up being extremely popular

with every woman but your wife if you keep that up," she warned him.

"It's a risk I'm willing to take," he told her airily.

The music ended and they strolled back to their table. Mavis, who was still seated with her friends at the other end of the room, gave them a cheery wave and then returned to her animated discussion.

Jack's eyes held a twinkle as he told Gale, "You can see that my wife is not jealous of you."

"I'm glad of that," she said.

"And if you weren't here I'd be sitting here alone."

"I doubt it," she said.

"We must meet at the pool in the morning," Jack said. "The weather report says fine and warmer tomorrow. There's nothing like this Maine weather after hot New York."

"That's your city, of course," she said.

"We live in Westchester but I commute to Wall Street every working day," he said. "During the summer I try to space the working days as widely as possible."

She laughed. "I don't blame you." For the first time in a long while she'd forgotten all her troubles and was beginning to enjoy herself.

"Mavis certainly bumped into the right

girl," Jack said. "I've been looking for a swimming partner."

"How long are you staying?" she asked.

"We are supposed to leave at the end of next week," he said. "But we may stay on longer. What about you?"

"I'm beginning a two-week stay. That is if I don't change my mind and go home."

"You mustn't do that," he said.

"It depends on how I adjust to the hotel."

"Where is home?"

"Hartford," she said, without going into details. Apparently the Pelhams had not heard about Emily's murder and she preferred it that way.

He asked, "When are you swimming in competition again?"

"I haven't any plans at the moment," she said.

"You'll want to wait until you're feeling more yourself," he said.

"Yes," she replied, without thinking.

At that moment Mavis rejoined them and in her boisterous way started the conversation on another track. She began telling about her golfing score which was murderously bad and the fun she'd had playing with the group she'd just been sitting with.

"Did you enjoy your dance with Jack?" she asked.

Gale smiled. "Yes. He dances very well."

"He enjoys it with everyone but me," Mavis assured her. "And that suits me fine because I'm one of those freaks who doesn't like to dance."

Jack told Gale, "You see what a perfectly matched pair Mavis and I happen to be."

"I'm impressed," she said.

They sat talking until after eleven. Then Gale excused herself since she was feeling very tired. The two saw her to the lobby of the hotel and she took the elevator upstairs while they strolled off toward the verandah. They were exciting people, she thought, but she couldn't say that she really understood them. There was something theatrical in the way they talked and acted, almost as if they were playing the roles of bright young moderns.

James had booked her an excellent room on the second floor with a view of the ocean, and she could hear the wash of the waves on the beach clearly. She undressed quickly and got into bed. Not until after she'd turned off the lights and was lying there staring up into the darkness and thinking about the evening did a strange thought suddenly strike her.

When she and Jack Pelham had been discussing her competitive swimming, he'd suggested that she probably wouldn't want to enter any more contests until she was feeling better. And she had been most careful not to tell him about Emily's murder and her subsequent shock and illness!

How could he know?

Did he know? Or had it just been a casual, meaningless comment? Possibly he had read something of her travail and been too considerate to mention it.

Perhaps these uneasy thoughts brought on the nightmare she suffered when she at last fell asleep. In it, Emily came to her bedside and tried to warn her of something, but no words came. Just a movement of her lips and no sound at all. Frustrated, Emily broke into tears, clasped her hands to her face, and then simply faded into thin air.

Gale dreamt that she was back in the family home in West Hartford. She was walking alone down one of the shadowed corridors when she heard her father's footsteps behind her. He was following after her. An icy hand of fear touched her shoulder. She turned around and there was a skeleton standing there behind her. She screamed as the skeleton advanced on her and suddenly the skeleton changed and became Jack Pelham, in his stylish summer suit. He smiled and took her in his arms and they began dancing as they had in the lounge.

But she feared him now. She was cold and rigid in his arms. And as they whirled along in the shadows he was transformed into a skeleton once more. She looked up into the grinning face of her ghostly partner and felt his bony arm around her. It was too much. She began screaming again — aloud, apparently, for she woke herself up with her frantic cries.

She was terribly ashamed of herself. If anyone in the adjoining rooms had heard her they'd consider her mad. Which, she told herself grimly, mightn't be too far wrong.

After a long time she fell asleep again and didn't wake until morning. After breakfast in the main dining room, she went upstairs and changed into her bathing suit and a beach robe. She gathered the suntan lotion, her small radio and the other items she might need in a beach bag and took the back stairway down to the patio and swimming pool.

She was just emerging out on the side verandah which was deserted when she saw a tall room-service waiter in white coat and black trousers coming out of the adjoining building. The waiter was carrying a tray and they noticed each other at precisely the same instant. A single glance told her that it was Rufe. Rufe, whom the police were still seeking, hiding out by working here at this summer hotel with the other college youngsters!

He went white when he saw her and turned and quickly ran down the steps and vanished around the corner of the hotel. She stood there on the verandah staring after him, her heart pounding wildly.

The next thing she knew she was walking on the beach in front of the hotel. She was close to the ocean, still wearing her beach robe and carrying the bag. She turned from the foam-flecked waves only fifteen feet or so distant to glance back at the hotel. And she saw that it was surely ten-minutes walk from where she now stood. How had she gotten where she was? There could only be one answer. She'd had another of her blackouts!

Panic seized her. She turned to hurry back to the hotel only to be confronted by a slender young man with red hair and freckles. His hair and swimming trunks were wet, as if he had just been in the ocean. "Hello!" he said.

"Hello," she replied nervously.

"You answered me this time."

"What do you mean?"

The young man was watching her with

shrewd blue eyes. "When I spoke to you before you walked by without answering."

"I didn't hear you. I wasn't feeling well," she told him, wondering who he was and what he wanted.

"You sure didn't look good," the young man agreed. "I could have sworn you were walking in your sleep."

"I'm all right," she said, ready to go around him. "I'm starting back to the hotel."

The young man moved to block her way. "Just a minute," he said. "Why run away before we get to know each other?"

"Please, excuse me," she said, trying to pass by him again.

But again he blocked her path. "My name is Larry Grant, I'm in law in New York and a guest of the hotel. So are you. I saw you in the lounge last night. You were dancing with that fashion plate, Jack Pelham. You're Gale Garvis, the swimming champion."

She gave him a despairing look. "Since you know all that why keep me here?"

"I wanted to meet you," he said. "I've admired you for a long while."

"Thank you," she said.

"The name is Larry, remember," he prompted her. "Larry Grant. And I prefer the ocean to the pool. Don't you dislike pools with all the hotel crowd cavorting in them like over-age seals?"

"I don't mind them," she said, hoping to get the conversation over with. She wanted to try and find Rufe.

"I do," Larry went on. "But I can see that you mightn't. I mean you've been used to swimming everywhere."

"Yes."

"You're going to the hotel pool now?"

"In a few minutes," she said.

He gave her a good-natured smile. He wasn't good looking but he had a craggy sort of charm. "Maybe I'll break a long-standing rule of mine and go up there and join you for awhile."

"I really must be on my way," she said.

He lifted his eyebrows. "Don't you want me to go to the pool?"

"I can't stop you, can I?" she asked him, annoyed at his delaying her. "It is there for all hotel guests."

Larry looked hurt. "That doesn't sound like a warm invitation, but maybe I'll come anyway."

"Suit yourself," she told him and she hurried by him and up to the path that would take her back to the hotel grounds. If Larry Grant was an example of the young bachelors at the hotel she could get along well without them. He struck her as being bold and inconsiderate. Surely he saw that she wasn't well.

Tears of frustration brimmed in her eyes. How humiliating that at the moment of crisis her nerves should have failed her and she'd succumbed to the blackout. She'd been having them at wider intervals lately and had begun to hope she was over them. Now she knew this wasn't so.

Reaching the hotel she avoided the patio and pool to head for the entrance to the kitchen. As she approached it she could hear the clatter of pans and dishes through the wide screen door, and above this noise the shouts of the help. The odor of breakfast bacon and coffee hung heavily over the area as she mounted the steps to the door.

A black man in chef's hat and white apron over white trousers and shirt came to the screen door to eye her suspiciously. "This is the kitchen, Miss," he informed her.

"I know," she said. "I don't mean to bother you. But I'm looking for someone."

"Who?"

"A young man. His name is Rufe or he may be using another name. He's tall with shoulder-length brown hair and he's working this morning as a room-service waiter."

The man listened to her stolidly. "I don't know," he said.

"What don't you know?"

"Whether we got anyone like that working here."

"But I saw him myself," she said, a desperate edge in her tone. "He has to be here."

"I'll find out," the man said and immediately vanished in the interior of the kitchen.

She stood there feeling helpless and even ridiculous. Suppose she did find Rufe, what would she say to him? What would she do about it? Would she turn him over to the police?

The man returned and informed her, "He ain't around."

"What does that mean?"

"He's just gone off duty."

"Where is his room? Would he be there?"

He shook his head. "He ain't in his room. I asked about that. He's like as not gone off with some of the other youngsters in a car or maybe down to the beach. He won't show up again until lunch time when he goes on duty."

"I see," she said, unhappily. "Thank you." And she turned and started back down the stairs dejectedly. She felt sure he'd gone a lot further than the chef had guessed. She was certain Rufe had skipped. She had lost her chance — and she still didn't know what that chance had been.

Chapter Five

The hotel pool was large — sixty feet in length and thirty-five feet wide. On either side of it double rows of deck chairs were set out for the hotel guests. At the far end, near the ocean, was the deep water with two diving boards and at the shallow patio end the life guard sat in a director's-type canvas chair.

As she approached the pool a figure in dark glasses and a Terry-cloth white robe sprang up from one of the deck chairs and came to greet her. It was Jack Pelham.

"I've saved a chair for you," he said. "Right next to mine."

"Thanks."

"You should thank me," he informed her. "I had some arguments doing it. Nearly every chair is filled this morning."

"I can see the pool is busy," she said, looking around at the crowded chairs and the many people of all ages frolicking in the pool.

"Too many around for comfort," Jack grumbled. "I thought you were going to stand me up. What kept you so late?"

"I had a bad head," she said. "So I went to the beach." It was true enough, as far as it went.

"The noise here isn't liable to help it any."

"I'll manage," she said. "I'm feeling better now."

"Good girl," he said, smiling at her with great charm. "Come and join me."

She went over and placing a blanket on the empty deck chair next to him stretched out on it. She took the suntan lotion from her beach bag and began to apply the mixture liberally to her body and face. "Where is Mavis?"

He was leaning on his side watching her from the adjoining chair. "Where would you expect? Over to the country club playing golf."

"Is that her daily routine?"

"Every day," he said. "That's why I'm glad you turned up. It's been mighty lonesome for me."

She was still busy with the suntan lotion. "I may not stay."

"Why?"

"Something happened this morning."

He looked concerned. "What?"

"Nothing really important," she said evasively. "It wouldn't mean anything to you."

"You consider me stupid?"

"No, not that," she said. "It was just something personal. It would have no meaning for you." She put the lotion back in the bag and settled down on the chair to enjoy the sun.

"You don't want to tell me about it?"

"No."

"Now you've hurt my feelings," he said. "I thought you looked on me as a friend."

She gazed up at his indignant face with a rueful smile. "I keep telling you — what upset me wouldn't have any importance for you."

He gave a deep sigh. "I know the act. Mavis uses it every so often. Feminine mystery! Okay, let it go at that."

"Thanks," she said.

"But you aren't really going to leave?" He sounded like a spoiled child.

To get him off the subject she said, "No. Not if it means so much to you."

"It does," he told her. "Believe me. I'm counting on you to brighten my vacation."

"Just let me rest quietly for a little," she begged him.

"Sure," he said. "We can swim later when it's not so crowded."

She closed her eyes with the cries of the swimmers and the splash of the pool loud in her ears. She had a vision of Rufe's pale, frightened face when he'd recognized her. And she could easily understand why he'd been so shocked. He must know the police were after him.

What should she do? Probably call James and inform him. Without any question her cousin would at once relay the news to the police. And even if Rufe had left, it would narrow down the range of the search and make it easier to catch up with him. She didn't think he'd get a fair trial, with James so sure Rufe was guilty. For all her love of Emily and her wish to see her murder avenged she couldn't bring herself to report her meeting with Rufe to James. She needed to wait and think.

The sun was warm and she drifted off into a light sleep. She had no idea how long she'd slept but when she opened her eyes and sat up to look around she saw that Jack Pelham was no longer in his chair. She decided he must have become impatient and left the pool when she suddenly spotted him standing with someone else by the railing at the far end of the pool, which overlooked the highway and ocean below.

The man he was talking with wore a somber dark suit of some silky material which shone in the sunlight and on his head there was a smartly styled brown straw hat.

His clothes made a striking contrast to Jack's white terry-cloth robe. The only thing they had in common was that they both were wearing dark glasses.

She continued to watch the two as their earnest conversation went on and it seemed to her that though the man in the black silk suit was tall and thin he was also much older than her new friend. She wondered idly who the stranger could be and what his business was with Jack.

Jack suddenly looked down the pool in her direction and must have noticed her sitting up. He said something to his companion and at once they both started walking back.

As they came nearer to her she saw that her guess had been correct. The man at Jack's side was considerably older with a lined face and prominent nose.

Jack came up to her with a smile. "So you've finally finished sleeping."

"I just dropped off," she apologized.

"You surely did," he said. "May I introduce a business associate, Mr. Frank Solon. He just flew in from New York."

The hawk-faced man was staring at her in a strangely intense way that made her uncomfortable. "Glad to meet you," he said in a harsh, somewhat uncultured voice. "I know about your swimming success."

"Thank you," she said.

He was studying her from head to foot in a manner which made her wish she was wearing more than her brief bathing outfit. He said, "You got a great body."

Jack showed embarrassment as he said, "Frank is an all round athletics man. He's owned a few boxers and wrestlers and has a part of a football team at present. He's strong for a healthy mind in a healthy body."

"You bet," Frank Solon rasped, still staring at her.

She tried to cover her uneasiness. "Have you come to stay at the hotel, Mr. Solon?" she asked.

"Passing through."

"Frank doesn't have too much time for play," Jack Pelham said. And she was aware of how nervous the man in black made him. He had lost all his easy assurance.

"Right," Solon barked.

"He's taking a plane back to New York later today as soon as we discuss some business," Jack explained.

Seeing her chance to be rid of both of them, she quickly told him, "Don't let me keep you from your business."

"I won't be ready to give Frank the information he wants until this afternoon," Jack assured her. "I'm waiting for a phone call from New York. I told them to page me out here. In the meantime I'm all yours."

"Sure," Frank Solon said. "I'll be going. See you later, Jack. Nice meeting you, Miss." And with a nod he walked on toward the hotel to vanish in the shadowed lounge.

Jack watched after him for a moment and then sat down on the chair beside her. She could sense his relief and wondered what it all meant. She had an idea he was afraid of the rather sinister Frank Solon.

She said, "He's a very strange person."

"Yes," was Jack's dry comment.

"And you're in business with him?"

"My firm handles some of his investments," Jack corrected her. He shrugged. "You know how it is. You get to do business with all kinds of people when you're in Wall Street."

"So it seems," she said.

"You didn't like him?"

She smiled bleakly. "He made me uneasy. To be terribly frank, he's sort of the Mafia type. The kind you always see playing a mob leader on television."

Jack gave her a significant look. "He's the real thing."

"Mafia?"

"Yes."

"And you look after investments for him?"

"All these fellows are dabbling in legitimate business today. If I refused his account there'd be a dozen other firms glad to handle it."

"I see."

"We understand each other and get on well," Jack said. "What goes on in his other world I don't care to know."

She studied him with a new understanding. "That's very convenient for your conscience, if you have one."

"That's saucy talk," he warned her.

"But then I doubt if you have one," she went on. "That handsome face of yours is much too manly and forthright to be genuine. You could operate in any kind of jungle."

"Thanks," he said with sarcasm. "There's nothing I enjoy more on a nice summer morning than having my friends cut me down to size."

She sighed. "Sorry. I had no right. I've only known you since last night. I apologize."

"Oh," he said. "So now you don't wish to be considered my friend?"

"I didn't say that."

"It amounts to it. You don't approve of my associates."

"I've told you," she protested. "We're practically strangers. What I think about you and Frank Solon shouldn't matter!"

"But it does," he said earnestly. "I want you to like me."

"Why should that matter?"

"To be utterly simple, because I like you. And Mavis thinks you're great. She's the one with the real class in our family."

"Please, Jack, let's drop it," she begged him.

"Not until I've told you all the facts," he said. "Mavis can't stand Frank either. She thinks he's cheap and awful."

"She could be right."

"Her father owns the firm and he's angry with me for taking on the account but it means a lot of money to me in commissions and I have a kind of pride, too. I don't want to be just the dummy son-in-law partner in the firm."

"You don't have to tell me all this."

"I want to. So you'll understand," he said. "I don't want you going around avoiding Mavis and me because of Solon."

"All right," she said. "I'll forget about it."

"You mean it?" Jack asked anxiously.

At that moment the young man she'd met on the beach came by in his bathing trunks. He smiled at her and said, "I've come to join you in that swim, Gale."

"Oh!" She was taken back; she'd not expected to see him so soon again.

"Who is this?" Jack said, rising with a look of sullen annoyance.

She stood up. "It's a friend who's staying at the hotel."

"Larry Grant is the name," the slim, red-haired man said, holding out his hand to Jack.

The handsome man hesitated, then shook hands with him and mumbled, "Jack Pelham."

"Nice to meet you, Jack," Larry said. "Come on now, Gale. You can't stall any longer. The pool is waiting."

She took off her beach robe and tossed it on the chair. "I'll see you later, Jack."

Jack looked angry. "This was to be our swim!"

"I beat you to it, friend," Larry said with a laugh as he led Gale to the pool steps.

She fastened on her bathing cap and told him, "He was right. I had promised to swim with him."

"You had lots of time and didn't," Larry said, descending into the water.

"I was resting," she told him, following him down the steps. The water was warm and pleasant.

The pool wasn't so crowded now and she was able to at once move out into the deep water and swim the entire length of it. All her old skill came back to her and she made it in record time. Then she clung to the edge of the pool as her red-haired friend laboriously followed her.

He was gasping as he reached her and caught hold of the pool side. "You shouldn't have made me rush that way," he said.

She laughed. "I didn't. I just swam at my usual pace."

"Another proof that women aren't the weaker sex," he said, still gasping for breath. "I really should have let you set the pace for your handsome pal."

Gale glanced back at the chairs where she and Jack had been enjoying the sun and saw that he had vanished. "He seems to have left the pool."

Larry gave her a teasing grin. "I'll tell you something. It wouldn't surprise me if he couldn't swim."

"Of course he can."

"Have you seen him in the water?"

"No."

"Well, don't be too sure. Those handsome guys can be terrible phonies."

Gale had already decided this, but she didn't want to admit it to this stranger. She said, "You oughtn't to say such things about my friends."

"Is he an old friend?"

111

"I know him and his wife."

Larry still clung to the pool side. "Long?"

"We met here at the hotel."

"Better be careful," he warned her. "Some of these friends you make at summer hotels can be a surprise."

"I'm not worried about Jack and Mavis," she told him.

"Good for you."

"And aren't you another summer hotel acquaintance?" she demanded. "If I follow your advice I'll have nothing to do with you either."

He winced. "You have a point."

"So?"

"So let's not argue about it," the young man said. "But I wouldn't count too much on handsome Jack and his missus. I mean I wouldn't mention them in my will or anything."

"Thank you," she said with a pert smile. "I'll race you back to the shallow end."

"You'll lead me back there," he told her. "You seem to have recovered from your sick spell on the beach."

Her face shadowed at the mention of it. "I'd forgotten about it."

"Sorry. That was clumsy of me."

"It was!"

"Well, pretend I didn't say anything about

it and get your satisfaction by beating me again. Say when!"

"Now," she told him, and with a bold stroke began to make her way back along the length of the pool. When she reached the shallow end she stood in the water waiting for him.

He appeared in a moment, gasping as he had before. "I'm no match for you at this," he admitted.

"You do very well," she told him. She found him pleasant in spite of his somewhat blunt manner.

They stayed in the pool for another fifteen minutes and then left it to stretch out on the beach chairs. Larry stared up at the almost cloudless sky.

"This is a lovely spot," he said.

"I agree," she said. "I almost didn't come here. But I'm glad I did now."

"Do you have a car?"

"No."

He glanced at her in surprise. "How did you get here?"

Somewhat awkwardly, she told him, "My cousin drove me."

"Don't you drive?"

"Yes. But I haven't been lately."

The red-haired young man gave her a cynical smile. "Did you lose your license?"

"No."

"I didn't think so," he commented. "You're obviously the law-abiding type. I can't imagine you getting a ticket for speeding."

"Really? How can you be so sure? You simply don't know anything much about me."

"I'm a shrewd judge of character."

Before she could think of a comeback, she saw Jack and Solon come out onto the patio at the end of the pool and sit at a table to order drinks. Jack was dressed in brown slacks and a yellow sleeveless sweater.

Larry was leaning on an elbow now and staring at the two. He gave a low whistle. "What do you know about that?"

She glanced at his lean, freckled face and saw a look of astonishment on it. "What now?"

"Your friend Jack doesn't pick his company very well."

"Why do you say that?"

He nodded toward Frank Solon. "Do you know who that is?"

"Yes. I met him earlier. His name is Frank Solon."

Larry looked grim. "And have you any idea what he is?"

"I understand he has Mafia connections if that's what you're making all the fuss about."

He swung his legs around and sat on the side of the beach chair with an earnest expression on his youthful face. "Frank Solon is Mr. Mafia himself. I don't practice law in New York City without finding out a few things. He's a very bad boy."

"Jack told me that."

"Oh, he did?"

"Yes," she said. "The reason he's friendly with Solon is because he is taking care of some investments. Jack is in Wall Street with his father-in-law."

"Is that so?" Larry Grant said, sounding interested. "I wonder what the name of the firm is. I've done some business with several Wall Street firms."

"Does it matter?"

"I suppose it doesn't," the young man said. "All I can say is I wouldn't want Frank Solon for a client."

"Jack has his reasons."

Larry Grant gave her a sharp look. "You don't seem to question anything he tells you."

"Why should I?"

"It might be wise once in awhile just on general principles."

She studied him with disapproval. "You have a very suspicious mind."

"Guilty," he said with a thin smile. "Put it

down to my legal training."

She put on her robe and gathered up her beach bag. "If you've finished maligning my friends I think I'll go in and take a shower before lunch."

Larry quickly got up. "I didn't mean to offend you."

"You're not very tactful, are you?"

"I want to be your friend," he said with evident sincerity. "I usually talk plainly to my friends."

She smiled bleakly. "Then I must qualify as one."

"Will I see you after lunch?" he asked.

"I don't know," she told him. "I haven't any plans yet." And she started to go.

"How about a putting contest? I think I can stand up better to you on the greens."

"I won't promise," she said over her shoulder and continued on along the pool.

She had to pass the tables to enter the hotel through the lounge. As she approached the table where Jack and Frank Solon were seated both men got to their feet.

Jack's smile was reproachful. "You didn't lose any time finding a swimming companion."

"He's hard to discourage," she said. "I hope you didn't mind." As she spoke she was aware that the eyes of Frank Solon behind his dark glasses were fixed upon her with embarrassing intentness. A cold, appraising gaze!

"It was just as well," Jack said amiably. "My call came from New York and I've had some things to discuss with Frank. We'll work the swimming in some other time."

"Of course," she said, uncomfortable under the icy surveillance of the Mafia chief and anxious to get away from the two.

"Mavis will be on hand for cocktail time," Jack promised. "Suppose we all meet down here in time for the music at six."

"All right," she said, ready to agree to anything just to escape.

Jack smiled. "Frank is fascinated by your swimming triumphs. Want to watch out or he'll be trying to get you under contract."

The man in the black silk suit showed no expression at all on his swarthy, lined face. But he said, "Good luck, Miss Garvis."

"Thank you," she said. "It was pleasant meeting you." And with a quick, forced smile she moved on. She *hadn't* enjoyed meeting Frank Solon and she'd been annoyed at the way he'd studied her. She'd felt naked under his cold gaze.

She went up to the lobby and used the

stairs to her room. After taking a quick shower and changing into one of the several linen dresses she'd brought with her, the problem of finding Rufe once again became uppermost in her mind.

Since it was lunch time she decided to inquire about Rufe from the captain in charge of her table. The dining room was not as busy at lunch since many of the guests had their lunch at the golf club or wherever they happened to be spending the day. After she'd taken her place and ordered, the elderly woman who acted as captain in her area came by to rearrange the small bouquet of wild flowers in the center of the table. Gale saw this as her opportunity to find out about Rufe.

"I'd like to give a message to a young man employed by the hotel as a waiter," she told her.

The thin, white-haired woman smirked knowingly. "What is his name?"

"His first name is Rufe. He has shoulder-length brown hair."

"You must mean Rufe Bradly. He's been working on room service."

"Yes. That would be him."

The woman nodded. "He should be in the kitchen now," she said. "I'll be going out there in a few minutes. And if he's around

118

I'll ask him to come speak to you when he gets a free moment."

"Thank you," she said. "I'd appreciate it."

Now she began to feel the strain of waiting. Her first course was served and she tried to do justice to it. Even though she was hungry from her morning at the pool she found it difficult to eat. She was almost trembling. So much depended on her seeing Rufe and talking to him.

She was toying with her main course when the captain came back to her table. "I'm afraid I won't be able to help you," the elderly woman said with annoyance.

She felt her heart miss a beat. "Oh?"

"Rufe Bradly isn't here anymore," the woman went on. "He left in mid-morning without notifying anyone. The chef had someone check his room and all his things are gone. So he has no idea of returning."

"He didn't even collect his wages?"

"He'd only have a couple of days coming to him," the captain said. "And he'd know they'd make a fuss about his leaving without notice. When they go they usually go this way."

Even though she'd expected something of the sort she was still badly let down. "Thank you, anyway."

"Glad to do it," the elderly woman said.

"We're short of help as it is. Every person we lose makes it that much worse. It's a continual battle keeping enough staff." And she moved away with this lament.

Did Rufe's running off indicate guilt or innocence, Gale wondered. And she still couldn't make up her mind. One thing was sure, she wasn't likely to get that close to him again.

After lunch she strolled on the front lawn of the hotel for a while, her thoughts still concentrated on Rufe. Then she went to the rear verandah. She was seated there staring out at the ocean when Larry Grant suddenly came out the screen door and seeing her, walked over to her. For a moment she'd hardly recognized him for he was wearing a sedate gray suit and black tie and white shirt.

He said, "I've been looking for you."

She smiled. "You're not dressed for putting."

"I'm not going to be able to challenge you to that match," the young man said. "I have to go back to New York."

"I'm sorry."

"So am I," he said with a sigh. "But the big boss called me. I'll be taking the plane from Portland this afternoon."

She gave him a surprised look. "Then

120

you'll be taking the same plane as Frank Solon. I understand he's flying back to the city today."

"That news doesn't exactly thrill me. How do you know he's taking that plane?"

"Jack Pelham said so," she informed him. "He said Solon wasn't interested in staying here."

"I can believe that," Larry said. "For one thing, there's no casino."

"He enjoys gambling?"

"He enjoys owning gambling resorts," Larry said. "I hear he has hotel interests in both Las Vegas and Freeport in the Bahamas."

Gale stood up with a smile. "You're remarkably well informed on him."

"No more so than any average New Yorker," the young man said. "Frank Solon turns up in the *Daily News* at least once a week." He held out his hand. "Sorry our friendship has to be so short."

She shook hands with him. "It's been fun knowing you."

"Even though I haven't approved of your new friends?"

"Yes."

"Good," he said, his face brighter. "Who knows? Maybe we'll meet again somewhere."

"It wouldn't surprise me," she said.

"And don't put too much stock in the Pelhams."

"I'll remember." She smiled. "Summer hotel friends are not to be taken too seriously."

He nodded. "Except me. Goodbye, Gale. It's been fun."

She watched him go back into the lobby with an astonishing feeling of loneliness. She'd known him no more than a few hours and much of that time he'd annoyed her with his comments. Yet she'd grown to like him for his frankness and she was sure she would miss him. It was strange that in such a brief period she'd come to feel she knew him well.

The balance of the afternoon was quiet for her. She felt lazy after a long day in the sun and found herself looking forward to joining the Pelhams at the cocktail hour. She needed some talk and excitement to cheer her up. Before she went down to the patio to join them she felt tempted to call James and tell him about having seen Rufe. Then she decided against it on the slim hope that she might through some mad coincidence encounter the hippie again.

Mavis and Jack were already seated at a table and having their first cocktail when she joined them. Mavis was wearing another smart summer dress in white with a bold black design across it and Jack looked every inch the wealthy playboy in a sports outfit in gray with a wine cravat to set it off.

"Here she is!" Mavis said with delight. "Do sit down, darling, while I tell you of my positively awful day on the greens."

Jack smiled as he helped Gale with her chair. "Mavis had such a bad score she'd rather have stayed here and helped me entertain Frank Solon."

"No I wouldn't!" his wife told him. "I can't stand that awful man." She turned to Gale. "And I understand Jack introduced him to you!"

"I didn't mind," she said quietly.

Jack had ordered for her and now the waiter came with her drink. Mavis gave her a warning look and said, "I may as well tell you that Solon has a roving eye for the ladies. You'd be better off not knowing him!"

Jack looked amused. "As a matter of fact he took an instant liking for Gale."

Gale was startled. "You can't mean that!"

"Sure," the handsome young man said. "He asked me a lot of questions about you."

She recalled the weird way the Mafia chief had stared at her and felt a chill of apprehension. She said, "He hardly said more than a dozen words to me."

Mavis looked wise. "Talk isn't his strong point, darling."

"Right," Jack Pelham agreed. "But don't be surprised if when you return to your room you find a dozen red roses and a message waiting for you."

She stared at the tanned, handsome man. "You're joking!" she gasped, but she had the uneasy feeling that he wasn't.

Chapter Six

The night maid usually turned down her bed and gave her fresh towels during the dinner period. And when Gale returned to her room around nine o'clock she discovered that the maid had also placed a long, cardboard box on the table for her. She approached it with almost a frightened feeling and when she opened the box she found it contained a dozen red roses. There was no card or message but because of what Jack had said she knew where they'd come from.

It was embarrassing. She hadn't liked Frank Solon and after what she'd heard about him she surely didn't want him interested in her. She could only hope she'd never meet the Mafia chief again. She felt it was unlikely that she would.

In the meantime she couldn't allow the lovely flowers to languish in the box. Unwrapping the tissue paper, she took the long-stemmed beauties in her hands — and an ugly, unexpected thing happened. From somewhere among the blooms an evil-looking, tiny spider emerged and moved

125

rapidly onto her bare arm. With an exclamation of disgust and fear she dropped the flowers and brushed the offending insect from her.

It all happened in a matter of seconds. The spider vanished and she reluctantly knelt down and picked up the fallen roses. Quickly she filled an empty water pitcher and placed them in it. Then she put the pitcher on a distant dresser which she wasn't using. The fragrance of the roses began to fill the room but the thing she most felt about them was repugnance that they had been a hiding place for the ugly insect. It struck her that this was in a way symbolic.

The Pelhams had asked her to join them in the lounge. After she freshened up a little she went downstairs to seek them out. They were at their usual table near the bar. As always they greeted her with warm enthusiasm. And soon she was listening to a long and complicated story about a cruise they'd taken in the West Indies.

When they finished Gale said, "You two seem to have been everywhere and to have done almost everything. Where do you find the time?"

The handsome Jack looked uneasy. "I have always believed in taking long vacations."

Mavis nodded. "And we divide our weeks off over the year. Father is very considerate in arranging this for Jack."

"One of the advantages of working for your father-in-law," Jack said.

Gale studied him with interest. "It's just occurred to me," she said, "that I'd never take you for the Wall Street type."

Jack raised his eyebrows. "Is there a type?"

"I mean, you don't give the impression of being a businessman," she went on seriously.

"What would you take him for?" It was Mavis who put the question to her. And this time she saw that the normally flighty blonde was serious and perhaps a little on edge.

Gale hesitated. "I don't mean to be disparaging but you are more like a theatre person, perhaps more the playboy type. You suggest what you were, a handsome photographer's model, more than what you are, a Wall Street businessman."

"What do you think of that?" Mavis demanded of her husband.

He showed a flush of crimson on his handsome face. "You mean, like the leopard I'm having difficulty changing my spots?"

"Probably you should be flattered," Gale assured him quickly. "Most of the brokers

I've met have been old, ugly and uninter-esting."

Mavis gave her husband an admiring look. "And Jack is none of those things."

"Nor am I to the manner born," Jack said with undisguised annoyance. "I never quite fit in at the exclusive luncheon clubs or the board meetings."

"Don't be silly, Jack," his wife protested, as if she saw some danger signal and was anxious to avoid trouble before it began.

"I meant nothing personal," Gale has-tened to add. "I think you have a suave, charming manner. You're certainly not a crude type like Frank Solon."

Jack's eyes met hers. "Speaking of Solon, did you get the roses?"

"Yes," she said quietly. "They were in my room when I went back after dinner. Of course there was no card or message with them."

"There wouldn't be," he said. "Frank doesn't operate that way."

"He must have liked you," Mavis told her. "He doesn't pay that kind of tribute to every girl he meets."

"I'm afraid they were wasted on me."

"Don't be too sure of that," Jack warned her. "Frank has a way of following these things up."

She frowned. "Please let him know as tactfully as you can that I'd prefer not to hear from him again."

Mavis spoke up. "I agree. If I'd been here this morning I wouldn't have allowed you to introduce Frank to this nice new friend of ours."

Jack smiled thinly. "No harm done. Gale is probably glad she met him, even though she doesn't want to be bothered by him anymore. He's a colorful character."

"He's a menace," Mavis snapped. "And you'll be sorry you took him on as a client before it's all over. Wait and see."

"I had to break in some new ground," Jack said. "Your father keeps all the accounts of his wealthy, socialite friends for himself." And he turned to Gale. "I find this table talk a headache. Would you give a fashion model a dance?"

It was evident that Jack was in a petulant mood. She was willing to dance with him since she felt this was her fault, but she hesitated in going off and leaving his wife alone at the table.

Mavis at once eased the situation by telling her, "Do dance with him, darling. I see some friends at the rear of the lounge and I want to do some table-hopping."

So Gale found herself on the small dance

floor with Jack once again, sorry she'd upset him and surprised that he was so easily hurt by her comments. For a successful businessman he was still very touchy about his photographer's model beginnings.

As they danced he gave her a wry look and said, "I have an idea you really have a very poor opinion of me."

"Why do you say that?" she asked, startled.

"You probably think I haven't any brains at all."

"Nonsense!"

"I don't know," the handsome man said thoughtfully. "I'll bet you have a lot more respect for that red-haired boyfriend you were swimming with. By the way where is he? I haven't seen him since noon."

"Larry?" she said. "He had to leave. His office got in touch with him."

"You said he was a lawyer?"

"Yes."

"Larry Grant," Jack recalled the young man's name. "I must keep him in mind. Find out what I can about him."

"I'll probably never see him again," she said.

"Just another summer acquaintance," Jack said in a teasing tone. And then he asked her, "Do you mind if we quit dancing for a little and take a stroll around the pool? It's a lovely night."

"That could be fun," she agreed.

He opened the door leading to the patio and they went out. It was a warm summer night with plenty of stars overhead. The pool was pleasantly lighted but there didn't seem to be anyone around. They went the full length of the concrete walk beside it to stand by the railing at the end overlooking the ocean.

"I'm really enjoying my stay here," Jack said, studying the lights of the pleasure craft far out on the water.

"I'm glad I came," she agreed.

He gave her a questioning look. "I've noticed a change in you since we met. It's almost as if you'd slipped off a dark cloak. Your mood is much more normal."

She sighed and stared out at the ocean to avoid his eyes. "When I came here I was under a dreadful strain."

"And now you're escaping from it?"

"I hope so," she said.

"May I ask what the problem was?" he said. "Maybe I can help a little."

"You've helped a great deal," she told him, her eyes still on the ocean. "You and Mavis have been good for me. But I'd rather not tell you about it."

"I see," he said, disappointment in his voice.

She glanced at him quickly. "It's not that I don't trust you or value your friendship. It's rather that what I've gone through has been so horrible I don't even like to talk about it."

His eyes found hers. "I'm sorry," he said sincerely.

"Thank you," she faltered.

And before she could in any way prevent it he'd reached out and taken her in his arms. He drew her firmly to him and kissed her on the mouth. He kept his lips pressed to hers for a long moment before he released her.

"To let you know I'm concerned," was his explanation.

She gasped in dismay. "You shouldn't have done that!"

"Why not?" he asked coolly.

"You've put me in a nasty situation. Suppose Mavis happened to see me in your arms?"

"She'd laugh about it."

"I doubt that!"

"Surely you know we don't keep each other on a leash," Jack said. "Mavis understands me and I give her plenty of freedom as well!"

Gale looked at him reproachfully. "I don't

care what your attitudes are. I only know if this happens again I can't go on being friends with you."

He shrugged. "I'm sorry."

"Then let's go back inside," she said.

"All right," he said with sigh. "There's no need for you to worry about what happened."

Needless to say she did. But Mavis was still with her other friends when they entered the lounge. And when she joined them at the table again she was in her usual, carefree, amusing mood. She apparently hadn't seen them on the patio and so no harm had been done. But Gale made up her mind never to allow herself to be alone with Jack again.

The days and nights went by and soon they were all due to leave the summer resort on the weekend. Gale had been in touch with James several times on the phone and he'd urged her to stay on a while longer.

"You sound ever so much better," he said.

"It has done me good here," she agreed. "But the friends I've made have to leave Sunday and I think I should go home too."

"If you're certain," he said. "Let me know Sunday morning and I'll drive up for you."

She promised that she would. It was a fact her health had improved. She had begun to think she was free of the frightening blackouts until she experienced a shock on the Saturday morning before she was due to leave the hotel. She and Jack had been swimming in the pool while Mavis was off to the country club with her golfing friends.

Suddenly there was a commotion on the beach below the pool. She and Jack went to the railing and saw a crowd gathering at a spot beside a high rock breakwater which ran from the beach out into the ocean.

Jack said, "I'll bet someone has fallen from the breakwater. People often walk out on it even though it's not too safe."

"How awful!"

"Let's go down and find out," he suggested.

She hesitated. "Should we?"

He gave her a searching glance. "Why not? I'd like to know what it's all about."

"All right," she agreed with some reluctance. It seemed morbid to go rushing down to the accident scene but she didn't want Jack to think her a poor sport.

A few minutes later she found herself on the edge of the circle of people on the beach. Jack, tall and imposing, had no trouble pushing his way through.

He asked, "What's happened?"

A worried youth in bathing trunks told him, "She fell off the breakwater and hit the rocks beside it. We've sent for an ambulance."

"She's alive?" Jack wanted to know.

"Yes," the youth said, "but she's hurt bad!" And he gave Gale a glance and moved back a little.

As he did she had her first glimpse of the outstretched bloody figure of the injured girl. And the sight hit her with a dreadful impact. She stared at the girl's bloodied face and body and in her place saw Emily! Nausea erupted in the pit of her stomach. She closed her eyes and turned away and began walking.

She was still walking but now she was in a different area of the beach, some distance from the hotel. Terror shadowed her lovely face and she stared straight ahead as she made her way along the wet sand close to the water's edge.

"Gale!" She heard Jack plaintively calling her name from behind her.

In a kind of daze she halted and looked around to see him hurrying up to her. "What got into you?" he demanded breathlessly.

"What?" she asked blankly.

"I was talking to those people about the injured girl and when I looked around you'd vanished. Then I saw you a hundred yards

135

away walking along the beach as fast as you could. It's taken me until now to catch up with you."

"Oh," she said vaguely. "I guess I felt ill."

"You could have warned me," he accused her.

"I didn't have time," she said. "Something came over me."

"All you had to do was touch my arm," Jack complained. "Speak my name. I'd have seen you were pale and understood."

She looked at him with distressed eyes. "I couldn't. I didn't have any warning myself." She hesitated, then decided to explain. "Since I've been ill I've had sudden blackouts."

His eyebrows raised. "Blackouts?"

"Yes. That girl, the blood, reminded me of something," she managed. "I reacted by fading into a blackout."

Jack looked distressed. "And you knew this might happen before you went down there? Why didn't you tell me?"

"I thought I'd be all right," she said unhappily. "I was beginning to think I was over those spells."

His handsome face showed a troubled frown. "I'm sorry. What about now? Feel well enough to walk back?"

"Yes." She said it without too much certainty.

His blue eyes were sympathetic. "I think we should go over and sit on those big rocks for a few minutes. Give you a little breathing spell."

"All right," she agreed, knowing it was a good idea.

He walked to the rocks with her and then spread out the towel he'd had hung around his neck for her to sit on. When she'd made herself comfortable he sat on the huge rounded rock beside her.

"You've never hinted to Mavis or me that you weren't in good health," he said.

"It's only this blackout business," she said. "I'm fine otherwise."

"You should see about treatment."

"I was in hospital," she said. "When I go back to Hartford tomorrow I'll make arrangements to see my doctor."

"How are you getting back?"

She sighed. "I'm calling my cousin, James Garvis, in the morning. He's going to drive up here for me."

Jack looked at her with serious eyes. "There's no need for him to do that. We'll be driving through Hartford on our way back to New York. We'd be glad to drop you off."

"I couldn't put you to that trouble," she protested.

"No trouble," he said. "I'm certain Mavis will be upset if you don't agree."

The idea both appealed to her and worried her. She wasn't anxious to have the two learn more about her personal affairs and yet she realized it would simplify things if she didn't have to ask James to make the long Sunday drive to Maine and pick her up. This was an ideal opportunity to get a lift home and probably be there earlier.

She said, "If you're positive it wouldn't be a bother."

"Not to drop you off," he said. "We couldn't stay for a meal or even for a talk. We want to push right on to New York. The later we get there the worse the traffic."

This fitted in well with what seemed best to her. If they'd leave her at the entrance of the house without coming in to meet James it would be ideal. It seemed she could accept his kind offer without fear of any more embarrassment.

She said, "I'll call my cousin and tell him I'll be coming with you."

"Good girl," Jack said approvingly.

"Later you must visit me in Hartford," she went on.

"Glad to," he said. "By the way, when I was talking on the phone with Frank Solon yesterday he asked about you."

She was at once a little tense. "I can't imagine why."

"He thinks you're a beauty. He often gets these crushes on young women."

"I hope you discouraged him."

He smiled. "I told him not to get too interested, that you had a red-headed boyfriend by the name of Larry Grant."

Gale blushed. "You didn't have to be that specific."

"It seemed to put him off," Jack said. "Do you feel well enough to walk back now?"

"Yes."

He helped her down from the rock and folded his towel and draped it over his shoulder. They began walking back. He said, "Mavis should be at the hotel by the time we get there. I'll tell her everything is settled."

When Gale returned to her room she decided to put a call through to her cousin. She reached James without any difficulty and told him of the offer the Pelhams had made. "It will save you coming up here," she concluded.

"I don't mind that," he said, sounding far away at the other end of the line. "You're sure you are satisfied to travel with these people?"

"Of course," she laughed. "We've been together most of the time for all the two weeks," she reminded him. "I feel as if I've know them for years."

He hesitated before he said, "Very well. But if there should be any delay in your leaving or any other change of plan let me know. I'll be worried about you."

"Unless you hear differently we'll be leaving by midmorning tomorrow," she said. "That ought to get us in Hartford shortly after one o'clock."

"I'll be expecting you," James said in his precise way. "Will you be bringing your friends in for a visit?"

"Not likely. They'll be in a hurry to continue on to New York."

"Oh?" James sounded somewhat put out by this news.

"They plan to come later and pay a regular visit," she explained.

"That would be very nice," he said, seeming more pleased. "You sound much better than you did. I'm glad the holiday has done you so much good."

"It has," she agreed. The account of her blackout on the beach only a short time ago could wait. "How are things at home?"

"The same," he said guardedly.

She sighed. "No word from the police?"

"No," James said. "I'm beginning to think

they've lost interest in the case."

"I hope not," she said.

"So do I. But they've not been able to find any trace of that Rufe. And he is the chief suspect as you know."

"I think they're wrong to concentrate on him," she protested. "It could have been anyone."

"Perhaps," James said dryly. "They don't seem to think so."

"We can talk about it more when I get back," she said.

"I'm not sure you should keep thinking about it," her cousin warned her. "You should concentrate on the present rather than on what happened."

"I try," she said. "It isn't always easy."

They talked for a few minutes more and then she hung up. She left the phone with a feeling of guilt. The police had slowed down their search for Emily's killer because they'd not been able to trace Rufe. She had known where Rufe was and had not told either James or the police. Now he had been gone from the hotel for days and it would be useless to inform on him.

It seemed to her she might always be haunted by the shadow of the tragedy. Had she been wrong in keeping silent? Or was she justified in doing so because of her conviction that Rufe was not the guilty party but merely an easy suspect for the police?

Saturday night proved to be a gala evening. In the excitement and rush of it she forgot her worries for a while. She danced with almost a dozen different men and they all sat in the lounge until after midnight when the caretaker turned out the lights. She went to bed exhausted and so was lucky enough to fall asleep at once.

Sunday proved a good day to say goodbye to the resort. It was drizzling rain and coolish. They were packed and on their way by eleven o'clock, with Mavis driving. Jack had complained of a hangover and asked to be allowed to ride in the rear seat.

"I may be able to get a little sleep," he groaned.

Mavis winked at Gale who was in the front seat beside her, saying, "He's always the life of the party at night but beware the next morning!"

"That's not fair," he protested.

"Don't argue, try to sleep," his wife advised him as they drove through the picturesque little village and across the bridge to the road leading to the main highway. She glanced at Gale. "How about you?"

She smiled wanly. "I feel a little tired, that's all."

"You didn't drink like my Jack," Mavis said.

They drove on until they reached the turnpike. By now it was raining so hard that it was almost impossible to see the road clearly.

"A regular downpour," Mavis said grimly as she drove. "Awful day!"

"I'm glad we're not at the resort still," Gale agreed. "We'd have so little to do on a day like this."

"You're so right," the pretty blonde said briefly. It was apparent she was feeling the strain of driving in the rain storm.

In the back seat Jack had apparently fallen asleep. They reached the turnoff for the New York turnpike at the juncture with 495. Mavis was talking little and Gale began to feel terribly sleepy. But she forced herself to keep awake.

At last they reached the Sturbridge area which meant they were about to leave Massachusetts and had only an hour's drive to Hartford. All at once Mavis left the turnpike to take a secondary paved road. A fairly winding, narrow road through a bush-lined, seemingly desolate region.

Gale turned to the woman at the wheel in surprise. "Why did you leave the main highway?"

Mavis looked grim, her eyes on the narrow road ahead. "The storm."

"I'd think it would be easier to drive on the main highway," Gale said. "Where does this road lead?"

"A shortcut."

"I don't know it."

Mavis replied curtly, "We've used it before."

Gale frowned. "I'd say it was leading away from Hartford." She didn't want to be unpleasant since she was their guest, but she felt Mavis had made an error and wished that Jack were awake to offer an opinion.

"It joins another road that goes directly to Hartford," Mavis said. She was driving very fast considering the heavy rain and the slippery road.

Beginning to know a real fear Gale said, "I think we should wake Jack and ask him about this."

"I'll manage on my own," Mavis said sharply without glancing at her.

Panic was setting in as Gale said, "I don't think you're doing very well. I wish you'd stop the car until we can decide if this is the best way!"

Mavis chuckled grimly. "It's the best way!"

Gale knew now something was definitely wrong. Frightened, she turned to appeal to

Jack to find him rising up behind her with a weird expression on his handsome face. Then she saw the cloth in his hand. As he pressed it across her mouth and nose she cried out and tried to fight it off, but was overwhelmed by the heavy odor of chloroform. She took a deep involuntary breath and passed out.

When she came to again her head was aching fiercely and she felt cruel, cutting ropes around her ankles and wrists which were bound behind her. A thick gag was tied across her mouth. She was in the back seat by herself and it was still raining. In the front seat Jack was at the wheel and Mavis was sitting beside him talking in low, earnest tones. She was still too dazed to hear what they might be discussing. She moved a little on the seat and managed a low, dull groan in spite of the gag.

Mavis at once glanced back at her. The blonde's face was lined with tension. And she said, "She's come to. Not that it will do her any good."

His eyes on the road Jack snapped, "Tell her to keep quiet!"

Mavis kept watching her. "You heard him! The less you struggle or try to talk the better for you."

Stunned and suffering, she stared at

Mavis with tears rising in her eyes. She slumped back against the seat, trying to control her nerves and make some sense out of her plight. She glanced out the side window nearest her and saw that they were no longer in the country but moving along some drab city street.

The rain was still coming down hard and there was little traffic. She wondered where they were and above all what this meant. And then the single, terrifying word, kidnapping, flashed across her mind.

No doubt Frank Solon was involved in this. The Pelhams had won her confidence and so trapped her.

Mavis spoke urgently to Jack. "We're due at the theatre by one."

"We'll make it," he said grimly.

"Solon won't like it if we're late."

"I've told you a dozen times already we won't be," Jack snapped angrily.

"All right, cool it," his wife shot back. It was easy to tell they were both extremely nervous.

Gale tried to move a little once again and almost slid down from the seat altogether. She gave another muffled groan that once more drew the attention of her captors.

From the wheel Jack shouted, "You'll keep quiet or get more chloroform. And I don't think another dose would do you any good."

Mavis glared at her over the front seat. "You're lucky to be alive," she said. "Remember that."

The cords at Gale's ankles and wrists hurt, and her hands were becoming numb. She stared out at the run-down street again. It was a city but not one that she recognized. The gray wooden and shabby red brick buildings provided no clues.

Nor did the neon signs. She read them dully without really taking them in — "Automotive Center," "Fine Food," "Newspapers-Tobacco," "Eat Here." They flashed before her in vivid yellows, reds and greens and meant nothing.

"Watch now," Mavis warned her husband. "You turn the corner and it's ahead on the right."

Gale began to get the feeling that they might be somewhere on the fringe of Manhattan. Perhaps in some dejected area of the Bronx. It had the weary, dirty air of a city, or rather the outer extension of some large city.

"Here we are," Jack said. And he swung the car around the corner so sharply Gale was almost thrown to the floor. She somehow kept herself on the seat though at an awkward, tortured angle. And now she saw a tall brown brick building with white stone trim and a huge sign hanging from its front, reading, "Orpheum." She recognized it as a large movie palace of the type found in every city in the old days. But by its dejected look it appeared to be no longer in use.

"The first alley," Mavis warned her husband urgently.

"I know," he retorted, and again he swung the car sharply.

This time Gale was a little better prepared. She braced herself as the car swerved into a dark alley, only wide enough for the car. They drove thirty feet and then Jack shut the motor off.

He now turned to take a look at her, a derisive smile on his handsome face. "What do you think of your friends?" he asked mockingly.

She could make no reply but she stared at him with all the defiance she could summon. She'd been a fool and they'd kidnapped her. But she would not let them have the pleasure of seeing how terrified she was.

Mavis was studying her and for the first time Gale was conscious of how hard the features of the attractive blonde woman really were. She couldn't imagine how she'd been able to accept them as wealthy people of background. They were obviously a pair of cheap crooks working for Frank Solon.

But they couldn't win! As soon as she was late arriving at Hartford James would be in touch with the hotel. When he found they'd left he would at once notify the State Police. After that it shouldn't take long until the search began for the Pelhams and their car. They really didn't have a chance to reap any big ransom for her, she told herself — not even with Frank Solon directing their efforts!

Jack said roughly, "We'd better get her inside."

Mavis nodded. "Yes. Try the basement entrance."

"Harry should have heard us and be here now," he said as he started to open the driver's door.

"Maybe he's on the bottle again," she warned. "And you know how crazy that makes him."

"Let's hope not," her husband said grimly and got out and went to a door with a dirty white light fixture hanging over it. The words "Stage Door" were painted on it. Jack pounded on the door impatiently, looking back at the car with an exasperated expression as he waited for it to be opened.

Gale felt a small ray of hope that something had gone wrong, that the door wouldn't be opened. But even as this went through her mind she saw it thrown back. Jack spoke to someone urgently. Then he came back to the car and opened the rear door.

"End of the trip," he told her as he grasped her in his arms and lifted her out. He carried her to the stage door and inside. There in the near darkness she caught a glimpse of an amazing figure. She first thought it was a child until Jack set her down on the basement floor and the tiny three-foot creature loomed over. When she looked up into his face she saw the wrinkled, evil face of an old man. An old man smoking a cigar and wearing a brown beret!

Chapter Seven

"This is Harry," Jack said in a mocking voice. "You and he will get to be good friends as time goes by."

The ugly midget chortled. "Yes, we will," he squeaked. "Yes, we will, indeed!"

It was the beginning of a nightmare. There in the murky, dank cellar Jack untied her ankles and wrists and took the gag from her mouth while Mavis and Harry stood by.

Jack instructed her, "Get to your feet. You'll be moving around on your own from now on." All the harsh cheapness that lay beneath his smooth facade was now apparent to her and she wondered how she could have been taken in by the two so easily.

Rubbing her wrists to restore her lagging circulation, she demanded, "How dare you do this?"

Mavis gave her a cold smile. "No need to play the haughty lady for us. If you want to get along here you treat us nice, see?"

Jack said, "She's right, Gale. We're still your friends and if you are smart you can make things easy for yourself."

She gave him a disgusted look. "Don't call yourselves my friends. I was a fool to trust you!"

The handsome man shrugged. "Go about it your own way. You may be here quite a while. But you'll have Mavis and I, not to mention Harry who is a great favorite with all the girls."

The little man took the cigar from his mouth and said, "That's the truth, Jack! I'm a regular ladies' man!" And he laughed shrilly.

Jack told Mavis, "Take Gale to her room." And to Gale he added, "A word to the wise. We're all armed. And all the windows of this place at the lower levels are barred. There's always somebody on guard at the exits. Because you haven't got a chance to escape you'll have a certain amount of freedom. Don't abuse it!"

Gale faced him defiantly. "As soon as my cousin finds out I'm missing he'll have the police after you."

Jack smiled grimly. "Don't count on it. Play it cool and you'll be safe. But any funny business and we have orders to shoot."

"So this is your gangster friend's game," she accused him.

He smirked. "Mavis will fill you in on the necessary details." And he nodded to the hard-faced blonde. "Take her away. I have some things to discuss with Harry."

The midget gave her an obscene wink and said, "We'll get acquainted later, honey!"

Mavis took her roughly by the arm and shoved her ahead of her. "Go on. We're taking the stairs to the auditorium."

Gale allowed herself to be led up a broad flight of stairs that came out in what had been the main lobby of the ornate movie palace. Its gilt and marble decor was now peeling and cracked, and the once majestic drapes of crimson velvet were soiled and shabby. The marble floor was strewn with waste of every description and in the shadowed atmosphere of the high-ceilinged place it seemed likely that rats might appear and scurry about at any moment.

Mavis paused for a moment in the middle of the lobby and stared about in disgust. "I don't expect this place has been used for ten years. And we have to be stuck with it for our headquarters."

Gale ventured, "It is Solon behind this, isn't it?"

"We'll save that until later," Mavis said derisively. "Come on. I want to show you this picture palace!"

This time she forced her toward an archway which seemed to open on complete darkness. But when they went through it Gale saw that they were in the wide, slanting orchestra section of the closed theatre. A single bulb on a stand in the middle of the otherwise bare stage threw some light around.

The smell of stale air and decay was again strong here. And as her eyes became accustomed to the shadows she saw that a number of the seats had been removed from the central section of the orchestra. This left only the bare sloping floor about three-quarters of the way up. No doubt the seats had been sold to some other building.

"In its day this was the show spot of the area," Mavis told her.

"Where are we?"

"Can't you just see me telling you that!"

Then she took her down the aisle to the orchestra pit. Stairs led from the pit to under the stage. Gale stumbled in the darkness on the narrow stairs but Mavis seemed to know her way perfectly. They came out at the rear of the stage and she had her first glimpse of the entire auditorium from the vantage point of stage center.

In addition to the huge orchestra section, there was a good-sized first balcony and a smaller second one. It was a vast theatre and high above everything was the projectionist's booth.

Mavis told her, "In the old days they used to have big stage presentations along with the movies. But that ended a long while ago."

"Why are you holding me here?" she asked her plaintively.

"I'll show you where you'll be living," the blonde said, ignoring her question completely. Taking Gale's arm again, she guided her across the stage to a dressing room at the left rear corner. There was a star on the door. "You're the star attraction so you rate this dressing room," the blonde jeered as she pushed the door open and turned on the inside switch.

The ceiling fixture was devoid of any shade and the two glaring bulbs revealed a good-sized room with a bathroom off it. There was a wide dresser with an elegant mirror now heavy with dust. A plain chair sat in front of it and there were easy chairs and a sofa in the room along with a folded screen in one corner. The dirty floor was carpeted in blue.

Standing between her and the door, Mavis said, "This is where you'll stay."

Gale looked at the woman who had pretended to be her friend. "Is this really a kidnapping?"

The blonde's eyes met hers coldly. "Yes."

"Why me?"

"You're well known and wealthy. Why not?"

Gale sat limply on the edge of one of the easy chairs. "You and Jack are professional crooks?"

"That's not a very nice description," the blonde purred. "Call us a couple on the alert for easy money."

"Are you sending word to my cousin, James Garvis, right away?"

"He'll find out."

"How much ransom are you asking?"

"None of your business. But I have a couple of things to warn you about."

"Such as?"

"Number one, watch out for Harry. That midget can be nasty and he carries a gun just like the rest of us. So be polite with him. He's a little touchy and maybe a little crazy as well."

She shuddered involuntarily. "You're not going to leave me here alone with him?"

"You'll be alone with him all right," Mavis said. "And then there's Malenkov. Now he's really batty. So watch out for him."

"Malenkov?"

"He's the caretaker officially. Used to be here years ago. Now he's hired to live here and watch over the dump. He may be loony but he's smart enough about a buck. That's

156

why he's working with us."

"Do you stay here?"

"Off and on. Personally I find it too spooky. But then you've got no choice."

Gale stood up again. "Can't we make some kind of deal?" she asked desperately. "I can get money for you and Jack. As much as you like. Just get me safely out of here and back home. I can promise my cousin will be generous!"

"Oh, you can?" Mavis asked with sarcasm.

"He'll pay you anything within reason and we won't try to tell the police. Just let me go free."

Mavis shook her head. "Not a chance. You must have been reading about thieves falling out. Well, I can warn you now, this bunch of thieves won't. We know what we want and our price for it!"

Gale stared at her in shocked disbelief. "You planned to trap me from the start!"

Mavis responded with grim amusement. "From the moment I collided with you and dropped my pocketbook, you hadn't a chance."

"How long do you plan to keep me here?"

The blonde shrugged. "That depends."

"On what?"

"A lot of things but mainly whether we get

what we want or not. We figure you should be worth plenty to us."

"I am willing to pay you whatever you want," she pleaded.

"No chance," Mavis said. "It has to be done our way. And remember what I told you about Harry and Malenkov." With this final warning she left the dressing room.

Gale hurried to the door but heard a key turn in it on the outside and when she tried to open it found that it was locked. Exhausted and filled with despair she took in her drab surroundings. The once brightly decorated dressing room was faded and dirty. Like all the rest of the mammoth movie house it had been too long neglected.

Who would ever think of looking for her here? Once James gave the alarm to the police, they would make a methodical check on hotels, motels and even lonely houses and summer camps. But here she was a captive in the center of some city, in a place no one would associate with a hideaway for kidnappers. The chances of her being found seemed dismally slim unless through some freak accident.

Slowly she made the rounds of the room. There was a single closet and the bathroom. Sickened by her surroundings, she sank down on the sofa and tried to keep control of her nerves. Having hysterics wouldn't help at a time like this.

She tried to fix in her mind what time it might be. Perhaps four o'clock? James would consider her overdue at this moment and if he hadn't already phoned the hotel he would soon be doing so. Then the search for her would slowly get into gear — not that she thought they would have any luck in locating her.

Frank Solon had been too smart in planning all this. And he must have been working on the idea long before she went to the summer hotel. He must have had an idea of where she'd be going and that she'd be alone. No doubt he'd followed the murder of Emily in the papers and from some contact with the servants in the big house had discovered her plans for a rest by the sea. Then he had gone to work.

Remembrance of Emily and the murder further upset her. It seemed they were both destined for violence and tragic deaths. Slowly she began to have the feeling that she was not meant to leave the old theatre alive, whether a ransom was paid for her release or not. It was a terrifying thing to admit, but she had to be honest with herself.

What to do besides merely wait? How to endure this? She had to go over the steps her kidnappers would likely take. First they'd notify James and tell him how much they wanted for her release. She could picture her cousin's shock, but she couldn't predict what his attitude might be. Only time would tell that. Of course he'd pay the ransom. He'd have to. What really troubled her was the fact she knew and could identify so many of the principals in the crime. How dare they let her remain alive?

Frightened as she was, she was still furious. The Pelhams had shamelessly exploited her loneliness and need for human contact. She'd been stupidly trusting, an accomplice to her own kidnapping. It was a lesson she'd never forget. But had she learned too late?

What about Larry Grant? He'd warned her about the Pelhams. If he'd not been called away from the hotel all this might not have happened. Larry had been keeping a close eye on her. When he saw the news of her kidnapping in the papers, perhaps he would get in touch with James and tell him all that he knew.

The police search would be bound to concentrate on the Pelhams. But would that be any help? She suspected that the wealthy young husband and wife team had been created especially for the occasion. With the kidnapping over they would change their identities completely and the Pelhams would vanish into the thin air from which they'd been created.

Her reverie was interrupted by sounds of the door being unlocked. She got up and stood watching tensely as it opened slowly. At first she thought it was opening by itself and then Harry showed himself. He had her bag and was laboriously dragging it into the room after him. Taking it as far as the table he let it go and gave her a sour smile.

"The others have left," he informed her, "so you answer to me now."

She took a step closer to the ugly, wrinkled old man in a child's body. "Then you can let me go! I'll pay you well!"

The midget laughed nastily. "They said you'd try and bribe me. It's no go, lady. Solon would have me dumped in the river with weights around my ankles if I tried anything like that."

"The police would get him!"

The midget continued to be amused. "You have to be joking. Frank Solon taken in by the police! You're badly mixed up, lady!"

"You'll never get away with this! Then what?"

The little man took a puff on the big cigar

he was smoking. And he cocked his head to one side and said pertly, "That don't happen to be my worry, Miss Garvis. You're one of those pretty, empty-headed fillies. You don't have any idea what you're up against yet."

Studying his freakish little figure in the murky light of the dressing room, she began to fear that what he said was true. She was caught in the web of an evil beyond anything she could imagine. It was futile to attempt coping with it. And yet her inner nature forced her to do it, though it made no sense.

She asked him, "Were you expecting me?"

"Sure," he said in his shrill voice. "Me and Malenkov got this bridal suite ready for you!" And he chuckled again.

"Who is Malenkov?"

"He's somebody you got to meet to appreciate," he jeered. "You're in for a lot of surprises here!"

She shook her head. "You're all mad!"

The smile vanished from his dried-up, elderly face and he said venomously, "You think I'm a freak, don't you?"

"What makes you have that idea?" she demanded nervously.

"I've had that kind of treatment all my life," Harry said contemptuously. "But when we get to a situation like this I have as

much power as you. See!" And he under-
lined his words by producing a menacing
gray automatic.

"I have nothing against you," she gasped.

"I got something against you," he said, his
little eyes bright with hate. "You're one of
the lovely normal people!"

"Please!" she begged him.

His good humor returned and he put the
gun back in his coat pocket. The sallow, old
man's features twisted in another smile.
"You don't need to be afraid of me. Just
treat me right and you have nothing to
worry about."

The warning Mavis had given her about
him came to mind. And she knew she must
handle him carefully. "Am I to be kept
locked in this dressing room?"

"No. You can wander around the stage if
you like. But don't try to escape. There'll be
somebody watching you every minute. You
may not see them but they'll be here."

She glanced around her apprehensively.
"It's such a dreadful, run-down old place."

"It used to be something special," Harry
told her. "I worked backstage here for fifteen years and every performer who came
here thought it was the best equipped
theatre in the East."

"What did you do here?"

He looked proud. "I was stage manager. We used to have special shows something like they have now at the Radio City Music Hall in New York. And I planned every detail of the staging and supervised its operation. On opening nights I'd go from dressing room to dressing room and knock on the doors to give them curtain warnings." He halted in his reverie and his wrinkled little face went sour. "That's all over with now. All the great days are gone. There's just Malenkov and I left. And half the time he doesn't know where he is."

She stared at the midget with alarm. "You mean he's insane?"

Harry chuckled. "You could call it that. You'll find out!"

"If I'm to be kept here, what about food and sleep?"

"I'm the chef around here," he said. "I get most of the stuff from a Chinese take-out place around the corner. You like Chinese food?"

"Not especially."

"You'd better get used to it," he advised her. "And you can sleep on that sofa over there."

She looked at the soiled, lumpy sofa and gave a tiny shudder of revulsion. "It looks filthy!" she protested.

"It's not the Waldorf but you'll manage," Harry said. "There's some blankets in the closet."

She decided on another attempt to reason with him. "If only you'd listen to me I could be out of here and you'd have all the money you asked for," she said urgently.

He shook his head. "I thought we understood each other about that. It's no use, lady. Solon makes the decisions here."

"Will he be coming to see me soon?"

"I'd expect so. He usually drops around when there's something interesting going on. I'll be leaving you for a little. And don't forget what I told you about your being watched."

"I'm not likely to forget," she said bitterly.

The little man left the dressing room and only partly closed the door after him. She stood there uncertainly. Everything she was discovering about this gloomy former movie palace made her more apprehensive. No one would think of searching for her in this place of cobwebs and shadows. It was a world as lost to the modern day as the ancient movies which had flickered across its screen and vanished. She was a prisoner in a phantom castle of another era.

She glanced about the shabby room which must have one day housed the greats of the entertainment world. Most of those names would be dead or in retirement. Time had passed them by as it had the once magnificent old building. It was a place of memories and ghosts!

The partly open door beckoned to her. Slowly she advanced to the door and opened it all the way. The stage was empty and silent with just the single work light out there to cut through the cavernous darkness.

Timidly she moved out by the light and stared into the grotto of the auditorium. The gaping area left by the removal of the many orchestra seats gave the lower section a peculiar appearance. She raised her eyes to the balconies with their curved rows of even seats, layer upon layer of them, and she imagined what it must have been like when they were all filled with people. What a thrill it must have been to step out on the stage then and know their applause. Now it was her prison . . . possibly the last place she'd know on earth. This grotesque cavernous monument to yesterday!

These somber thoughts were suddenly interrupted by a sound which struck terror in her heart. From high above her on the right came a peal of loud maniacal laughter. She glanced up in horror as the thunderous music of an organ playing a mighty overture began. It filled the huge, darkened theatre and throbbed painfully in her ears. Automatically she pressed her hands tight against her ears to shut off some of the majestic clamor.

At the same time her eyes searched in the shadows above for the source of the weird outburst of organ music. After a moment she saw a thin, bald man seated in an alcove at least forty feet above the stage on the right, located between the stage and the box seats of the upper balcony. High up there in this recess he swayed over the keyboard of an organ whose speakers apparently were located at various levels around the stage.

This must be Malenkov, she decided, the official caretaker of the old theatre. In spite of the insane loudness of the music it could not be denied that he was an accomplished organist. And it struck her that at one time he might have been associated with the theatre in this capacity.

The bedlam of the overture ended abruptly in a confusion of chords that drained away to a pathetic sobbing sound. Then there was silence followed by another mad burst of laughter. Looking up at the alcove she now saw the fantastic bald man leaning over the railing smiling at her. In an instant he'd vanished and she heard a whirring, mechanical sound from the same side of the stage.

As she watched the odd sound ended and a door in the black side wall slid open to allow the mystery organist to step out onto the stage not far from her. He had used a special elevator to come down from the organ loft. No doubt this had been in regular use in the days when the organ music had been part of the theatre's offering.

He came directly to her, a scarecrow figure in a tattered dark gray topcoat, shirt collar open and tieless, face grimy and unshaven and wisps of gray hair falling wildly around the fringe of his domed bald head. He had a long, lantern-jawed face with sunken, mad eyes. As he approached her with a grin on his wasted features he pointed a skinny forefinger at her.

"You liked it?" he queried her in an old man's wheezy tones.

She was finding the organist even more frightening than Harry. "You startled me!"

"You didn't know the organ still worked? That the music was still there?" the old man exulted. "They've locked this place up but they couldn't kill its soul!"

"You are Malenkov?"

"You know my name," the weird old fellow exclaimed. "Did they tell you?"

"Yes."

"Once I was famous," the weird old man said. "You've heard of Jesse Crawford, the wizard of the theatre organ? Well, I was thought better than him by many!"

"And now you're the caretaker here?"

He nodded. "Not a suitable post for me, you understand," he said glancing around furtively as if someone might overhear him. "But it allows me to remain here with the organ. I can still give my concerts. Only the rats and the cockroaches may listen to them but I have that small satisfaction."

Gale was trying to find out who else might be in the theatre besides Harry and this strange old man. Carefully, she said, "Well, there are a few who hear you."

The lantern-jawed face was bleak. "There's those two, the ones who work for Solon. But they're away as much as they're here. She don't like me or my playing. And there's Harry, if you want to count him. And of course the others!" A crafty gleam had come into his sunken eyes.

"The others?"

He glanced furtively around again before he leaned closer to her and whispered, "You know who I'm talking about!"

"I'm afraid I don't," she said, hoping against hope that she might be on the verge of making some important discovery.

169

His mad, sunken eyes met hers. "The ones who don't talk."

"Oh?" Did Frank Solon employ deaf mutes as well as midgets?

"Yes," Malenkov went on with satisfaction. "The ones who wait in the shadows and listen. They appreciate my music. They know what it means."

"Who?"

He hesitated slyly. "The ghosts!"

In the midst of her disappointment she felt a chill of fear. "The ghosts?"

"It's true. There are times I can't sleep for their crowding in around me," Malenkov continued. "I sleep in one of the dressing rooms under the stage. The ghosts keep coming in and waking me. And then there's Elena! She knocks on the door of each dressing room every night!"

"She knocks on the dressing room doors!" Gale repeated. "Who is she?"

"You don't know about Elena?"

"No."

The old man ran a hand over his bald dome. "It was a tragedy," he said. "Harry had this crazy crush on her."

"The Harry who is here now?"

"Yes, the midget," Malenkov said. "Elena was the star dancer in all our special stage shows. We had our own chorus line right

170

here and only the star acts traveled to come here and be featured in the shows."

"And she didn't return Harry's interest in her?"

The old man looked scornful. "She told him off!"

"I see," she said quietly.

The mad old organist drew his tattered coat around him proudly. "Of course she was in love with me!"

"And?"

The long face became grim and haunted. "He waited for his chance and killed her."

She stared at him. "Surely not?"

"That's what he did. He was the stage manager here, and he waited his chance to get even," Malenkov went on sadly. "And he found it. In most of the spectacles we used a rising platform that came up from under the stage." He pointed his scrawny finger down at the grimy floor of the stage. "You can see the edges of it, almost where you're standing now."

She stared down at the stage with startled eyes and moved back a little. She thought she saw the joins of the platform but with the accumulated dirt couldn't be sure.

The mad organist chuckled. "You needn't be afraid. I don't think it's been used in years. The whole mechanism must be rusty and seized up by now."

"What does the rising platform have to do with your story?" she asked him.

"Elena was always the star of the shows. She'd do a special dance after the overture. I mean a solo dance. Then the chorus would join in. Well, in this show she was to come up as a mermaid from under the sea. And she stood on the platform for her entrance. Harry had charge of it and he somehow figured it out so he made it halt with a jerk when it was part way up from the cellar. It sent Elena sprawling and half-off the platform. Then he started the mechanism again fast so that it came straight up and she was jammed between the platform and the stage. You could hear her shrieks all through the auditorium. The theatre was full for a holiday afternoon show. The orchestra and the chorus were numb with horror. Nobody moved or did a thing and her cries of agony went on!"

Gale whispered, "Oh, no!"

"And then my cue light showed. Harry was signalling me to play to drown out those screams. He had the audacity to ask me to help him cover up the horrible thing he'd done. So I played, louder than her screams, and I watched as they lowered the platform and then the rest of the show went on. As soon as I could I went down to her. But she was dead by the time they got her off the platform."

"It's a dreadful story!" she gasped.

The bright, mad eyes met hers. "Most people think so."

"Surely Harry was punished for what he did?"

"For an accident?" The weird old organist demanded in a scornful voice. "How could you blame a poor midget for something that was beyond his control? He simply told them the mechanism had jammed and then suddenly freed itself. And who was there who could prove him at fault?"

"But you say you knew he did it deliberately!" she protested.

He offered her an insane smile. "Did I say that? Now that was very wrong of me! Not at all fair to my little associate. We share the responsibility for this fine theatre together these days. We are the best of friends!"

She shook her head. "I don't understand."

The old man laughed softly. "You shouldn't try. It is the only way one can manage. And of course it helps to have Solon's extra money."

"Are you on Solon's payroll, too?"

He smiled. "Frank Solon is a very generous man."

She stared at him for a long moment, then said, "Do you realize he has me here as a prisoner? That I'm being held by his henchmen?"

He seemed not to hear her. His sunken eyes were directed at the blackness of the empty auditorium. "There is one thing I should have added about poor Elena. Harry did not escape completely. For every night she comes to the door of the dressing room where he sleeps and knocks on it. I wait for her nightly visit. She knocks on all the dressing room doors!"

Chapter Eight

Malenkov walked away slowly from her to vanish in the shadows of backstage. She was alone once again.

Touring the backstage, she paused before the complicated electrical board and wondered if any of the switches remained in working order. Then she wandered on to the ladders that led straight up to a gallery over the stage in which scenery was stored. She strained to peer up into the dark heights and pick out the catwalk. Great bags of sand ballast were used to balance the scenic pieces and allow them to be easily drawn up out of sight.

She crossed the stage to the elevator to the organ loft, and saw another door that went down to the orchestra level. Her heart began to beat rapidly as she debated her chances of losing herself in the orchestra and waiting until one of the several exits were unguarded to make her way out. It was surely worth a try!

She glanced around to be sure no one was watching her. Seeing no one, she quickly went down the stairs. Then remaining close to the wall of the theatre so she'd be lost in the shadows, she made her way up to the rear of the orchestra section. An eerie silence had returned to the vast auditorium following the mad organ music.

At the back of the theatre she looked about nervously for some further place of refuge — perhaps a closet or small anteroom where she could hide for a little. She saw a door directly ahead of her and decided to try it.

She guessed that it might have been the office of the theatre manager in the old days. Quickly she tried the doorknob, it turned easily. In an instant she had slipped inside and closed the door after her. The room was shrouded in darkness, but she had no desire to turn on a light. Her chances of remaining hidden were better in the dark room.

Like the rest of the theatre the room had a heavy odor of stale air and dampness. She pressed tightly against the wall hardly daring to breathe and hoping that she'd not been seen. The next move would be to escape from the building.

By remaining in the office for a while she would know whether she'd been missed or not. She would have to leave before Harry returned with food for her. The vision of his ugly little face terrified her. She was sure he was capable of great evil.

From a distance away in the darkness she thought she heard a door open and close, but she didn't think anyone had entered her hiding place. Still, it increased her tension and made her more wary. She'd about decided she was safe when she heard a rustling in the pitch dark behind her.

A chill of fear raced down her spine. She was not alone; she could not risk remaining in the dark with who-knew-what threat. She started for the door.

But a hoarse voice in the doorway ordered, "Stand back!"

She recoiled from the strange voice with its menace and wheeled around in the darkness.

Now from almost at her side, a higher-pitched voice cried out, "Don't let her go!"

Bewildered and sick with fright she turned in another direction, sure that the room was filled with her enemies.

And from just in front of her a weird falsetto voice taunted, "She likes the dark! Put out her eyes!" A crazy laugh followed in the same voice.

"No!" she screamed, in spite of herself. She had given her location away by speaking out, but she was beyond caring.

"Stay where you," the first hoarse voice ordered her from the doorway where she'd heard it earlier.

A whisper came in her ear. "Get her!"

She was on the verge of sobs that could not long be held back. The shrill laughter came from directly in front of her once more and she halted.

"Stop it!" she sobbed. "Stop torturing me!"

At the same instant the room was flooded with light. Harry stood grinning below the light switch.

"You!" she gasped, glancing around the room to locate the others.

"You were warned not to try any tricks," the midget said.

"Who helped you in this?"

His wrinkled, sallow face showed triumph. "You mean the other voices?"

"Yes."

"Mine," he said with satisfaction.

"Yours?"

The little man nodded. "Yes. I was in vaudeville before I became a stage manager. I was a ventriloquist. I had more voices at my command than most of them and I could place them anywhere as I did just now. I fooled you, didn't I?"

"Yes," she said in a low voice. "Yes, you

managed very well."

"What did you hope to accomplish by coming in here?" Harry asked. "You haven't a chance of getting to the exits."

"I thought I might."

"Silly girl," Harry said. "I hope you've learned a lesson."

"I have."

His evil little face showed amusement. "I know you've met my associate Malenkov. I heard him playing for you."

"You're all mad!"

"I wouldn't say that." The midget spoke calmly, the gun in his hand covering her. "We look at things with a different viewpoint from you, that's all."

"Where are the Pelhams?"

"The Pelhams?"

"I suppose that's not their names," she said wearily. "I mean the two who brought me here."

"You mean Jack and Mavis," he said. "They're probably meeting with Solon. He'll be glad to know they managed to get you here."

"When will they be back?"

"Probably not until morning," Harry said. "Why should you worry? You have Malenkov and I to keep you company."

"And the ghosts," she said grimly.

Harry grinned malevolently. "Did he tell you that story? But of course he would. He's never gotten over losing his beloved Elena. Funny part is he claims I was to blame."

"Weren't you?"

The midget glared at her. "That's something I don't care to talk about," he said. "Now head back to the stage."

She meekly left the room and went down the aisle to the stage and the star dressing room in the corner. When she went inside the dressing room the little man gave her another nasty smile.

"Maybe I'd better lock you up for a little," he said. "You don't seem to take advice very well."

"I'll stay here," she said.

"You'll get in serious trouble if you don't," he told her. And then he left.

The dressing room door had not been locked but she was certain the midget had posted Malenkov or someone else outside to guard her. He wasn't apt to trust her again. She began to pace up and down restlessly wondering what was happening in Hartford. Surely by this time James would have called the police in. But she knew the chances of their coming upon this theatre hideout were small.

She began thinking about Emily and what

had happened to her. And of Rufe! She wondered where he'd gone. Wherever he was the shadow of Emily's murder still hung over him. And she was almost positive that he hadn't been to blame. Otherwise she wouldn't have kept silent about his being at the summer resort. But her judgment of the Pelhams had been so faulty that she could also be wrong about Rufe.

She could picture James' distress at discovering her missing. He would now blame himself for not coming to meet her, even though she had persuaded him not to drive to Maine and pick her up. But he would only think of his failure to make the trip. And he would add it to what he believed was his laxity in allowing Rufe to remain in the house and Emily's resultant murder.

And if she weren't found alive, James Garvis would go through life feeling responsible for the deaths of her sister and herself. Frank Solon would undoubtedly have his henchmen collect a reward for her and then toss her murdered body out along a highway somewhere. She'd read of cases like it but never dreamed that one day she would find herself the victim in one of them.

Her head was aching and she sank into a nearby chair. She was still sitting there when the midget returned with some cartons of food in a paper bag. She stared at him in dismay for she realized that for a time she'd experienced another blackout, a mild one, but still a lapse of memory. This brought back the old terror.

The little man put the bag on a table and told her, "There's plenty of food and some coffee there. We want to keep you healthy."

"Is that so important?" she asked bitterly.

Harry eyed her coldly. "It makes no difference to me," he said. "But we have orders from Solon. I guess the boss must have a crush on you."

Her cheeks crimsoned. "That's ridiculous!"

The little man chuckled. "You'd be better off if he had."

He left her again and she opened up the bag and took out the cartons of Chinese food, hoping there might be an address on the cartons which would give her an idea of where she was being held captive. But Harry was too smart to make that error. The cartons were plain ones.

The food was good enough, but she had little appetite. However the coffee was strong and revived her a good deal. Again she began worrying about what was going on outside this nightmare place in which she was a captive. How long would it be before

Solon sent a ransom note to James? Surely when the story broke it would be on radio and television but there were no signs of either radio or television in the old theatre.

After a little she ventured out onto the stage once again. As she'd expected there was someone watching for her out there. It was the mad old organist, Malenkov.

He was seated in a folding canvas chair, still in his ragged topcoat. "You gettin' tired of this place?" he suggested.

"Yes."

"You'll be here a long while yet."

"How do you know?" she asked.

"Harry says so."

She frowned. "Why do you listen to him? He's not your friend. He was responsible for the death of your Elena."

"How do you come to know that?"

"You told me!"

"I did?" he seemed suddenly vague.

"Yes, only a little while ago. You described the accident and blamed Harry for it."

"He *did* kill her!"

"Then why don't you break with him? Let me out of here and I'll see you get enough money to be independent. You won't ever have to come back to this theatre or your menial job here again."

The organist got up. "I don't want to leave

the theatre or my organ up there. If I left here I'd have nothing to live for."

"I'd expect you to hate this place!"

"It's my only link with Elena," he said. "I can't leave here." He stared at her oddly. "Did I tell you what Elena was wearing that night she was killed?"

"No," she said impatiently. "Why do you torture yourself talking about it?"

"Because I remember it so well," he said, his sunken eyes lighting at the thought. "Elena was dressed all in gold that night. She was supposed to be a queen from the bottom of the sea. She wore a dress of gold and a golden cape. I can still see it glittering under the lights, just as plain as the night it happened. And when I went to her afterward the cloak was all stained with blood on the inside." He bent his head and was silent for a moment. Then in a choked voice, he added, "I fainted. When I came to she was gone. They'd taken her away."

Gale looked at him sternly. "You feel so badly about your lost Elena. What about me? If I'm kept here I'll almost certainly be murdered."

Malenkov seemed startled by her words. "You're too young to die."

"That's what will happen just the same," she insisted, moving nearer to him. "I'll die unless you help. You can't do anything but mourn your lost Elena but you can save me!"

He rubbed his beard-stubbled chin as he considered this uneasily. "No," he said, at last. "No. I can't help you. They'd find out and kill me."

"Not if you left with me," she reminded him. "They wouldn't be able to harm you."

Malenkov backed away from her fearfully. "Don't talk like that! You can't escape it! I can't help you! Look out!" His last two words of warning were pitched in a different, louder tone.

She didn't know what he meant. But she suddenly found out. The floor on which she was standing began to revolve at a dizzy rate and a huge spotlight flashed blindingly into her eyes. And from a distance, in the wings where the electrical board was located she heard the midget's high-pitched laughter!

Lifting a hand to shield her eyes, she plunged forward in an attempt to seek release from the spinning section of floor on which she'd been caught. As she did so the momentum of the spin threw her heavily to the hardwood floor of the stage.

As she lay there groaning, the spotlight moved to her again. Harry laughed uproariously at her. She raised herself up and saw that he was on a small platform by the electrical board causing all these things to happen to her.

He turned off the spotlight. "I had to stop you from tempting Malenkov somehow," he told her as he nimbly came down the platform steps. "The revolving section of the stage and the spotlight seemed the best answer."

"I could have broken an arm or leg," she said angrily.

"I doubt it," the midget said. "You're much too young and supple. I'm not too old to appreciate a lovely body you know."

"I'd rather deal with Malenkov or the others than you," she told him.

His sallow, wrinkled face showed disdain. "You dislike me because I'm more than a match for you and you wanted to regard me as a freak."

"Why are you so touchy about your size?" she asked.

"People like you have made me this way," he told her.

"It's your own bitterness you see reflected in others," she warned him.

He came closer to her and reached out a small hand to take hers. "Are you telling me you want to be more friendly?" he asked with an insinuating smile.

"Don't touch me!" She backed away in fear.

He eyed her scornfully. "You soon changed your tune."

"I don't want you near me!" She turned and fled back to the dressing room, slamming the door shut after her. From outside on the stage she could hear his mocking laughter. And she knew the warnings she'd had about him were not to be taken lightly.

She remained in the dressing room as the night went on. Eventually she found herself falling asleep in the chair she'd sat in since her hasty retreat from the menacing midget. And she decided she would have to attempt sleeping on the sofa, regardless of how distasteful it was for her. She went to the closet and got out the soiled blankets folded on the shelf there and placed them on the sofa. She made no attempt to undress but removed her shoes.

Everything seemed quiet outside. She guessed that someone might be stationed out there to keep watch on her, but that Harry had left. She carefully pulled a chair in front of the door to act as a brace against it and also to warn her should anyone attempt to enter during the time she was asleep.

Only then did she turn off the lights and return to the sofa to get between the blankets. In spite of being uncomfortable and afraid she fell asleep almost at once. How long she slept she did not know. But she awoke with a start.

And what had wakened her was a soft knocking on her door. At once the ghost story recounted to her by the mad organist came to mind. Cold terror surged through her as she stared into the darkness and heard the knocking repeated.

She was fully awake. And at the second gentle knocking she began to wonder if rather than a ghost this might be someone come to her assistance. Overcoming her fear, she threw aside the covering blankets and got up from the sofa, then stealthily crossed to the door.

There was no further sound out there. Very carefully she drew the chair away from the door and then cautiously turned the knob and opened it a little. The night light still burned at center stage and close to it she saw Malenkov in his tattered coat, slumped in a chair. He had obviously fallen asleep. And the intruder had not wakened him.

Her curiosity further aroused, she opened the door wider and stared out into the shadows. It was then she saw it! The ghostly figure standing at the very rear of the stage, beckoning to her.

Gale was caught in a horrible dilemma: whether to remain a captive probably doomed by her kidnappers or attempt an escape with the aid of a ghost. Telling herself that the beckoning figure, whether dead or alive, could do no worse than Solon could, Gale forced herself to venture out onto the shadowed stage. She was in her stocking feet so the chance of waking Malenkov was slim. He seemed deep in sleep.

As she moved forward into the shadows she strained to catch another glimpse of the phantom female figure. But the ghost had moved on, and for the present was lost to her. Frightened but driven by her desperation Gale went on into nearly total darkness.

Still there was no sign of the phantom. She began to think it had been an illusion or perhaps imagination on her part. That once again she'd reached a dead end. And then she heard a deep sigh from beside her.

She turned and saw the phantom looming in the darkness beside her. But this was no lovely Elena who waited there. It was a horror almost beyond her comprehension. In the brief glimpse she had of the ghost she saw a blotched, distorted female face, hair long and wildly askew, clothes tattered and faded like shrouds from the grave. A specter who even smelled of death and decay. And who now thrust out a bony, skeleton hand to grasp her.

It was too much! Gale screamed and backed away. As she did so two things happened in the same instant. The ghost vanished and Malenkov awoke and fired a shot in the direction of her scream barely missing her.

She swung around crying, "Don't shoot! It's only me!"

The old madman came hobbling toward her, gun in hand. "What are you doing out here?"

"The ghost," she managed tautly.

"Elena?"

"Maybe."

The ancient Malenkov was bent eagerly toward her, all interest. "Tell me about it."

She swallowed hard. "There was a knocking on my door."

He nodded. "It happens every night. All through the theatre."

"I came out to see who it was."

"Go on."

"I saw a figure in the shadows. It beckoned to me. You were asleep. I went to join it." She halted in her account.

"Then what?" the old man asked irritably.

She hesitated. "I don't know." She didn't want to tell him of the horror she'd seen.

Better to play on his emotions, make him think it had been his beloved Elena who had summoned her.

She finally said, "I got close to her and then I became afraid and screamed. You know the rest!"

Malenkov gasped. "It was Elena come to help you and you scared her away."

"What's going on here?" The question came in Harry's shrill voice. And the tiny figure of the midget advanced toward them in the darkness, a flashlight in his hand. He directed the beam on Gale and the organist.

She quickly said, "I had a nightmare."

"What are you doing out here?" Harry demanded curtly.

"I wandered in my sleep," she said. "I screamed and he fired a shot at me."

"I heard it," the midget said irritably. He turned to Malenkov. "Is that what happened?"

He nodded. "She screamed and I fired at her."

"You're lucky he missed you," Harry told Gale disdainfully. "He's a remarkable shot for his age and condition. Then Solon would have been upset."

"Why?" she taunted him. "He can collect for me dead just as well as he can for me alive."

"Smart, ain't you?" the midget said sarcastically. "Now suppose you be smart enough to go back to your room so we can all get some sleep."

She slowly crossed the stage and went into the dressing room. She heard him turn the key in the door and knew she was locked in for the night. Under the circumstances she was just as glad. At least the spectral figure she'd seen couldn't get in. Or could she? Why not, if she were a ghost? Unnerved by the thought, Gale left the light on in the dressing room for the balance of the night.

She slept fitfully and when she saw by her wristwatch that it was nearly nine in the morning and time to get up she threw aside the dirty blankets and hastily made her way to the bathroom to wash and freshen up. Her dress was wrinkled and messy looking from sleeping in it and her hair was also dishevelled. She did what she could to make herself presentable.

All the while she thought about the happenings of the previous night. She was convinced she had seen a ghost — if not the lovely Elena's, surely that of some other phantom that haunted the ancient theatre. One thing she'd noted was that Malenkov had not contradicted the lie about sleepwalking she'd offered the midget.

This suggested the old man might be switching to her side, perhaps because he believed firmly it was Elena's spirit who moved about in the old theatre in the after-midnight hours. In time he might accept it as an omen and decide to help her after all.

And what about James and the police? By this time James could well have had a first note demanding ransom for her. And the police must be conducting a search for her at this very minute. Once again she wished she had some idea where she was. Surely it had to be some city between Hartford and New York. But where? She was mulling this over when she heard someone moving about in the room outside.

Opening the bathroom door, she discovered Harry with a breakfast tray. The evil-looking midget gave her a glance of displeasure. "Trying to make yourself attractive for my benefit?" he asked sourly.

"Hardly," she said, having decided the only way to cope with him was to be as bitter in manner as he was.

He showed mild surprise. "At least you're being honest."

"I wish I could say the same for you and your friends."

His smile was sour. "Captivity brings out the best in you. Here's some breakfast.

You'll be having callers soon."

"Who?"

"You'll find out."

"If you know, why don't you tell me?" she wanted more information.

His wrinkled face wore a malicious look. "I think it should come as a surprise."

"I hope it's the police."

"Not likely," the midget said derisively.

"This place won't be that hard to find," she said, angling for a clue to her location.

Harry showed no uneasiness. "They'll never locate you here," he said. "And if by some mischance they should close in on us I have orders to be sure you're not taken alive."

"How nice of you to tell me. Especially when you're so reticent about other things."

"You're playing brave," he taunted her. "And you're shaking in your shoes."

"You think so."

"I know it," Harry said with a derisive expression on his sallow little face. "And I know you weren't sleepwalking last night."

"Oh?"

"You were trying to sneak away again and lost your nerve."

She forced a stiff smile. "That's an interesting theory."

"It's what happened," he retorted. "Too

bad Malenkov didn't put a bullet in you. You need that kind of lesson."

"You told me last night that Solon wouldn't like to see me shot. Are you changing your story?"

"No," Harry said. "Solon wouldn't like it but I'd be pleased."

"I'll remember that," she promised.

"Enjoy your breakfast," the midget said mockingly and he went out on his short, bowed legs.

She sat down before the tray knowing that he hated her enough to kill her coldly at any time. He hated all normal people, she thought. To him she was a representative of that other world he could never enter.

The breakfast consisted of watery orange juice, some burned toast, margarine, cheap marmalade and bitter, grind-filled coffee. It struck her that preparing her breakfast had been less than a labor of love for the little man. But she made herself eat some of it realizing she must keep up her strength.

With the beginning of this second day of her captivity she was starting to formulate a plan. It would depend on her winning at least some aid from the mad organist. And that was a touchy business. But if she could manage that, she might still escape.

She was just finishing her coffee when the

door opened and Mavis came in. She looked weary and her face was lined by strain. She studied Gale with appraising eyes.

"You seem to be doing all right," she said.

Gale asked, "Do you care?"

"No," Mavis said. "But someone else might."

"Why don't you let me go before the police find me here and you're all in trouble?" she asked, rising.

Mavis laughed. "You're kidding!"

"I won't give evidence against you if you give me a chance to escape," she promised. "I'll pretend you and Jack had no part in my kidnapping."

"That's real nice of you," Mavis said. "But I'm not interested."

"You'll regret it."

"Maybe," the blonde said. "But don't count on it. I can still see you sitting there at our table in the hotel lounge so grateful to have friends. That was a laugh."

"You did take me in," she admitted bitterly. "But then I was lonely and ready for it."

"Making a play for Jack," the blonde jeered.

"You're wrong about that," she corrected her. "It was Jack who made the play for me."

"So you say." The girl looked just a little bothered.

"Don't think he's so devoted to you," Gale told her, following the idea up. "If I'd gone along with his ideas maybe this would all have turned out different."

"I don't believe you," the blonde said hotly. "What would Jack see in you?"

"Enough."

"Don't try to play games with us," Mavis warned her. "You're in plenty of trouble right now but you can always have a bit more."

"Is that a threat?"

"With you here in this position I don't have to threaten you," the other girl said with disdain.

Gale eyed her solemnly. "I wouldn't want to have to live with your conscience."

"I manage very well," the blonde said.

"Are you my visitor for the morning?" she asked.

"Just one of them," Mavis jeered. "The most important one is on the way. Just to prove we're going to take the best of care of you we have a doctor coming to give you a checkup."

Chapter Nine

There was something in the way Mavis said this that sent a chill of fear through Gale. What dreadful thing were they planning to do to her now? Why should a doctor be coming to see her? The very mention of it had a sinister sound.

"What are you talking about?" she demanded nervously.

Mavis studied her with those cold blue eyes. "You'll find out."

"You're telling me this to frighten me!"

The other girl smiled. "If that's so it's working. You're trembling."

And she was. Not only with fear but from frustration. She hated herself for having been such a fool as to be trapped by Mavis and her husband. She should have listened to James' advice and been careful making friends with strangers.

She said, "Things may not go all your way."

"I'd be willing to bet on our chances," the hard-faced Mavis told her. "Too bad your skinny, red-headed friend left so suddenly.

If he'd stayed on we might not have been able to get you to drive with us so easily. Especially if he'd offered to give you a lift back to Hartford."

Gale could at least agree with the blonde in this. If Larry Grant hadn't been suddenly called back to New York she might have driven back to Hartford with him. She said, "When the papers tell of my being kidnapped he'll remember you two and tell the police about you."

"There'll be nothing in the papers," Mavis said. "It's part of our deal. Your cousin says nothing to the police or press until we're paid off."

"I don't believe it."

"You don't have to," Mavis said. "I'm telling you what's going on."

"James wouldn't be tricked by you that way," she exclaimed. "He's bound to go to the police. I know him!"

Mavis smiled blandly. "We tricked you easily enough."

"James is a different story."

"You'd be surprised."

The door opened and Jack came in, still looking every inch the wealthy playboy in his smartly fitted sports outfit of light brown coat and dark brown trousers. He gave Gale an interested look and then told Mavis,

"Leave us alone. I want to talk to her."

The blonde showed annoyance. "Why do I have to go?"

"Because I say so," was Jack's quietly menacing answer.

Mavis frowned. "That's no reason."

"It better be if you're wise," he told her, his handsome face dark with anger.

"What goes on between you two?" Mavis asked suspiciously.

"Are you crazy?" Jack snapped. "I've got some things to discuss with her and I don't need you. Now get!" And he grabbed her by the shoulders and pushed her out through the door. Mavis left with some angry protesting. He closed the door on her loud comments.

Coming over to Gale wearily, he said, "Women! You can never count on them."

She smiled. "So it seems."

He eyed her suspiciously. "What were you telling her?"

She pretended innocence. "Why do you ask that?"

"Judging by the way she acted you've been working on her jealousy," he said. "She may not be as smart as you but let me tell you she's a whole lot more vicious. I wouldn't taunt her if I were in your shoes."

"In my shoes does it matter?"

200

"Maybe not," he said. "I want to prepare you for a few things. First, Solon will be here to see you this morning."

"I don't want to see him," she said.

"You have no choice."

"Thank you."

"And there's a doctor coming to examine you," he added, confirming what Mavis had told her earlier.

She tried to cover her fear by frowning and saying, "What are you bringing a doctor here for?"

"You'll find out," he said stolidly. "And by the way, don't try to tell any wild stories to the doctor. He knows who you are and why you are here. He works for Solon like the rest of us."

"He must be a fine doctor," she said with disgust.

"He was until he got mixed up with peddling narcotics," Jack said with a grim smile. "Since then he's learned to compromise when Frank Solon thinks he should."

She eyed him with contempt. "He destroys and corrupts everyone he comes in contact with. You and Mavis and those two madmen you've left me here with. And now this doctor!"

"We all share common interests and motives," Jack said. "You'll gain nothing by fighting against what's happening. You'd be wise to cooperate."

"Cooperate in my doom?"

"You make it sound so dramatic," he said with contempt.

"What are your plans for me? How much ransom have you asked for my safe return?"

"Enough."

"You daren't let me go free. I know too much. I can tie you all in with the kidnapping. Solon and the rest of you."

He looked at her directly, his eyes cold. "You're telling me that even when the ransom is paid by your cousin we daren't send you back to him alive."

"Yes."

"You've missed a subtle possibility," he said in his suave way. "There is another alternative."

"What?"

"We could safely return you alive as agreed upon for the ransom money provided you aren't coherent."

"Not coherent!" she echoed him in a startled voice.

"Yes. We all know you've been upset mentally since your sister's murder. It's a question whether you've been entirely coherent since then. And surely it's a matter of record that you've suffered from those blackouts."

She was beginning to understand why a doctor had been sent for. They were planning to do something to her mind. To turn her into a kind of vegetable who would offer them no threat.

"You couldn't!" she gasped.

"We could," he said slyly. "And we may. It depends on what Solon decides. He has an interesting future planned for you no matter what happens."

She backed away from the handsome man whose cruelty and ruthlessness now showed clearly on his tanned face. "I won't see that doctor!" she exclaimed. "I'll lock myself in the bathroom!"

"It's an old door," Jack said. "We'd have no problem breaking it in."

Terror melted her show of defiance. "You can't lend yourself to anything like this," she said piteously. "Help me!"

He eyed her stonily. "I've already given you the best advice I could. You'll be ahead of the game if you don't fight every step of the way."

"What can you expect when you're bringing a doctor here to destroy my mind?"

"That's not why he's coming," Jack said. "At least that's not his purpose in coming here today. He's simply going to give you a thorough checkup."

"Why?"

"Frank Solon will tell you."

"I don't believe you're telling me the truth," she said, edging toward hysteria again. "You're keeping the facts from me."

"No," he said.

There was a knock on the door and he gave her a meaningful glance. "Remember what I said. Cooperate." And with that he went to the door and opened it to a thin, nervous man of young middle age whose distinguishing features were a gaunt face and horn-rimmed glasses. "Come in, Doctor," Jack said.

"I had trouble finding this place," the doctor said nervously as he entered.

"That's the way it should be," Jack told him.

The doctor paid no attention to Gale at all but gave Jack a searching glance. "Where is Solon? He's supposed to meet me here."

"He'll be along."

"I hope so," the gaunt man said uneasily. "I'm expecting a package from him and I need it badly."

Jack winked at him. "You've got some anxious clients waiting, I guess."

"Don't be funny!" the doctor snapped.

His bag still in hand he turned to Gale for the first time. "Is this the girl?"

"Obviously," Jack said. "We don't kidnap them wholesale."

The man in the horn-rimmed glasses glared at him again. "And may I further remind you, I'm not in the mood for your dubious humor."

"Right, Doctor," Jack said with an indulgent smile. "This is your patient, Miss Gale Garvis."

The doctor came over to her brusquely. "I have a brief examination to make and some questions I want to ask you."

"What sort of examination?" she asked.

He arched an eyebrow. "Nothing to disturb you. Heart, lungs, blood pressure. The usual sort of thing."

"Why?"

"Someone has an interest in how healthy you are," he said.

"It seems I haven't any choice about this," Gale told him bitterly.

He opened his bag and brought out his stethoscope. "You're right, you haven't," he agreed grimly. And he at once went about making the routine examinations he'd mentioned.

Jack was standing across the room from them, studying the pages of a magazine. She endured the various tests, still on edge, and wondering what it was all leading to.

"Now a family history," the doctor said bringing out a pad of paper and ballpoint pen. "What about diabetes? Lung disease? Heart attacks?"

"This is madness," she protested. "What does it matter? Solon will likely have me murdered after he collects the ransom money. Why is my health suddenly so important?"

"I'm here to ask questions, not answer them."

Jack put aside the magazine. "He's right. Give him the answers he wants," was his order.

And so she replied to the long list of questions. None of it made any sense to her and she began to have a gnawing fear that the questions were merely a trick to confuse her. That the real purpose of the doctor's visit was to determine her mental state, to give him a chance to decide what means to use to render her harmless to her captors.

When he finished with the questions he took a hypodermic from his medical bag and turned to her with it in hand. "I have one more test," he said.

She shrank away from him. "I'll not be injected with anything!"

His gaunt face showed annoyance. "I'm not planning to inject anything into your veins," he snapped. "I merely want to take a sample of your blood. It is important that I have it typed correctly."

"Why?" she demanded nervously.

"Part of my interest in your health," he said. "This won't take a minute."

He filled the glass tube with her blood then swatched the spot with alcohol. "That's all," he said. "I won't bother you anymore." As he returned the various items to his bag, he asked Jack, "Why isn't Solon here?"

"Probably he is," Jack told him. "He wouldn't come down here right away. You can go to the office on your way out."

"I haven't time to wait," the doctor said. "I made this visit as a special favor to him and he should show his appreciation by being here on time."

Jack smiled bleakly. "You can always depend on Solon to return a favor. Don't worry."

"We'll see," the doctor said and he went on out.

She was left alone in the dressing room with Jack again. Now she crossed to him and asked, "What did all that mean?"

"Don't be so impatient," he said. "You'll

find out soon enough."

"Are you afraid to tell me?"

His handsome face was set in hard lines. "What you need to know you'll find out from Solon." And with that he turned and followed the doctor out.

She stood there troubled and bewildered. Events were taking a turn she did not wholly understand. But she was beginning to put the pieces of the puzzle together. Kidnapping was an extremely risky undertaking. And Frank Solon would be anxious to avoid all the pitfalls if possible. Rather than murder her, he would return her in a state in which she could not give evidence against the members of the kidnapping gang, including himself.

Since it was known she'd suffered from mental problems, including her several blackouts, Solon was undoubtedly planning to have her mind destroyed. She would leave the old theatre a vegetable unable to explain what had happened or who had been responsible. But to all intents and purposes she would have been returned unharmed. The mental trouble would be blamed on a breakdown rather than on deliberate tampering.

This had to be the answer. There could be no other reason for the doctor coming to visit her.

As she went over all this in her mind the dressing room door opened and Frank Solon came in. The gangster wore a blue, pin-striped suit and light straw hat. Dark glasses concealed the expression in his eyes, but his hawk-face was grim as he came to stand before her.

"You afraid?" he asked.

"Yes," she said frankly.

"No need," he said in his harsh, brusque way. "Matter of business. The ransom note has already gone out."

"Have you had any answer?"

"Not yet." His very presence gave off an ominous vibration.

She stared at him fearfully. "Why did you have that doctor examine me?"

"I want you in good shape."

"That's not all, I'm sure!" she protested.

He regarded her stolidly. "You got any other ideas?"

"You intend harming me in some way."

Still he showed no expression. "Don't worry about it!"

"They'll know if you hurt me," she warned him. "When the doctors check on me after I'm returned they'll find out what you've done. And when the police get you it will be worse than if you had merely murdered me!"

His swarthy faced showed a jeering smile. "You got a lot of imagination. Save it!"

Gale shook her head. "You're even more evil than I thought!"

He brushed this aside with a weary gesture of a carefully manicured but hairy hand. "You're comfortable enough here. We could have treated you rough. What's the complaint?"

"Thank you for your kindness," she said bitterly.

"I'm not trying to be funny," he warned her. "You're being treated with kid gloves."

"Left at the mercy of two madmen!"

"Harry and Malenkov are okay as long as you do what they tell you," Solon said. "This is all going to be taken care of neat. No one is going to lose his head and if your cousin listens to reason you needn't worry."

"I don't believe you!"

He scowled at her, then surprised her by moving across the room and throwing himself down in the single shabby upholstered chair.

Looking up at her, he said, "You talk to me like I was some kind of animal."

"Animals are seldom so deliberately vicious!"

"You been acting like this since you first saw me at the hotel. You acted then like I was some kind of dirt."

"I distrusted you and rightly," she said, not understanding this new mood.

"I'm a human being," he said angrily. "I'm just like everyone else. I have a wife and a daughter. My girl is about your age."

"How would you like to have her kidnapped?"

The inscrutable black glasses were fixed on her. "She could be at any time. I got enemies like everyone. Maybe I'm more careful to protect her."

"I'm sorry," she said. "I can't see you as a husband or father."

"You think I've got no feelings?"

"That's right."

"Maybe you don't know as much as you think," the hawk-faced man said, rising from the chair. "Maybe you don't understand me at all."

"I think I do."

"Think whatever you like," he said. "But don't do anything foolish. I want you to stay healthy. And Harry is kind of strange. He might like to have an excuse for harming you."

"You could still let me go," she said. "I've promised to say nothing."

He shook his head. "There's no chance of that." And he turned abruptly and left her.

The meeting with Solon had told her nothing; she'd gained no new information at all. She'd have to go on waiting and worrying.

She remained in the dressing room after the Mafia chief had gone. And eventually Harry came to her with sandwiches and coffee on a tray. The little man gave her an evil smile. "Your lunch," he said, putting the tray down.

"I'm not hungry," she told him, remaining in her chair.

The midget shrugged. "I don't care whether you eat it or not. I have orders to serve it."

"Where are the others?"

"Everyone has gone except Malenkov and me," he informed her. "So you'd better be nice to us."

As she spoke the organ outside began to be played loudly. She said, "Evidently Malenkov is in a musical mood again."

"Better get used to it." Harry chuckled. "I've known him to go on for hours."

"He plays well enough but too loudly."

"He was the organist here in the old days," Harry said. "But he's crazy now."

"That's a pretty general state around here," she suggested.

The midget looked amused. "You could

be right. You and Solon have a good talk?"

"Yes," she said sarcastically. "He told me you'd let me leave after lunch."

"Sure," Harry said with a laugh. "You remind me about that."

When Harry left she ate one of the sandwiches and drank some coffee. The organ music outside went on with hardly a break. It began to get on her nerves, and she finally walked out onto the stage. The single work lamp gave off the only light and she found herself wondering what it was like outside. In the big, shadowed building it was always night and there was no way of checking on the weather.

Her wristwatch told her it was around two in the afternoon. She moved slowly around the stage thinking of the morning's events and trying to formulate some plan for escape. There must be a way. There had to be!

Here in this nightmare place of madness and phantoms she must wait and watch for the right moment to make a break for freedom. It was possible that she might fail. But better to fail than die or lose her mind in these squalid surroundings.

She glanced up to the organ loft and saw the bald Malenkov swaying over the keys, blissfully unmindful of anything but his music. She wondered how much of his story about his lost Elena was true and how much fantasy? One thing she was positive about was that the old theatre indeed did have a ghost. She had seen the macabre creature in the night and would not soon forget her!

Now she went over to the door of the elevator leading to the organ loft. And out of curiosity she pressed the control button. After a moment the elevator door opened revealing the small carriage. On an impulse she decided to get in it and see where it took her. She had an idea it might stop at other levels beside that of the organ loft. She touched the inner control button and the door closed on her. There was a tiny overhead light in the elevator which gave off a murky glow. She felt the mechanism vibrate and there was a humming sound as the elevator ascended.

It came to an abrupt halt and then the door automatically opened again. She stepped out into the organ loft. Just in front of her the bald, emaciated Malenkov was bent over the organ. When he saw her his sunken eyes showed surprise and fear and his claw-like hands lifted from the organ keys. The music faded abruptly.

"I'm sorry I surprised you," she apologized.

He was staring at her. "For a moment I

didn't recognize you," he said. "I thought it was Elena."

"Why should you think that?"

He studied her in haunted fashion. "Sometimes she does come to me here," he said in a low voice. "She comes to me when I'm playing. I never tell Harry because he wouldn't believe me."

"I understand," she said.

The sunken eyes brightened. "I believe you do."

"You can be certain of it. You have my sympathy."

The old man lamented, "They treat me like a fool because I'm reduced to being a caretaker. I'm better than any of them!"

"Of course you are."

"Harry is the worst," he said in a hushed voice, crouching over the organ in the semi-darkness of the loft. "He enjoys humiliating me! He always hated me!"

She said, "Last night I saw the ghost. But I didn't tell him."

"No use," the emaciated Malenkov agreed. "He'd only call you mad!"

"But I did see her. That's why I screamed."

He nodded eagerly. "And I awoke and fired at you. I remember."

"Yes."

"Nothing personal, you know," the madman said. "I have a job and I must do it. Otherwise Harry would soon see they got rid of me."

"I understand."

"So you saw my Elena?" He was all excitement.

"I saw a ghost," she agreed. "And I would suppose it was she. I couldn't see all that clearly."

He nodded his dirty bald head. "I know," he said. "It's that way with me sometimes. All I see is her blurred figure. The face is hidden completely."

"I think she came to warn me," Gale said. "She knocked on my door and that was what woke me up."

"I told you she would."

"I remembered."

A crafty look came over his beard-stubbled face. "She comes to Harry's door every night and knocks on it. He's terrified but he won't admit it. He knows it's her ghost and she does it to punish him."

"She goes all through the theatre?"

"In corridors you've never even seen," Malenkov said. "She moves like a shadow in forbidden places. And one day she will wreak her vengeance on that wicked little man."

Gale said, "Harry says I'm watched all

216

the time. Is that so? Are there others here in the theatre besides you two?" It was vital for her to know this if she planned to escape.

He leaned toward her in the shadows. "I don't know," he said. "I've seen others. But maybe they're ghosts. It's hard to tell anymore."

With a sigh she moved over to the rail of the loft and gazed down at the stage. The height made her a little dizzy.

"You're very high, up here," she said.

"Yes," Malenkov agreed. "Especially when you look straight down."

As she studied the stage below and the auditorium with the gaping area left by the removal of the orchestra seats she spotted a tiny figure moving down the aisle toward the front of the stage.

"That must be Harry," she whispered.

The organist came to join her, peering short-sightedly down into the dark cavern. "I can't see," he complained.

"It's Harry all right," she said. "I must go down. He'll be looking for me."

"And he won't want you up here," the organist agreed.

"I'll take the elevator at once," she said, and she hurried across to it. She intended to ask him if it stopped at other places than the loft and the stage level but she didn't take the time to do it now.

Pressing the control button, she waited for the door to close and the cage to begin descending. At last it reached bottom and she got out. But to her surprise she was not at the stage level but apparently below it.

She stepped out of the elevator into a long, shadowed corridor with doors opening off it at intervals on both sides. Annoyed that she had missed the stage level she advanced cautiously along the corridor looking for a stairway to use.

She'd gone only about half the length of the corridor when she heard a movement in the darkness behind her. She wheeled around quickly with fear on her lovely face and saw nothing. But she was convinced that someone was lurking there in the shadows.

She remembered the mad Malenkov's comment about it being hard to separate the ghosts from people in the deserted old theatre. And now, her heart pounding, she worried whether it was a ghost or a human who was stalking her there in that lonely place.

Fear made her move on quickly and then she heard the sound again. This time she uttered a cry of dismay and plunged toward the nearest door. It opened easily to her touch and she went in and slammed it closed after her. Then she leaned against it sobbing with fright.

The blackness of the room in which she found herself was not comforting either. And she worried that she might have gone from one danger to another. Feverishly she groped for the light switch. After a long moment her hand came in contact with it and she pushed the button. With relief she greeted the murky light emanating from a single yellow bulb hanging from a cord from the ceiling.

Now, her body still pressed against the door, she took in her surroundings. It was a dressing room in which costumes had been stored. An unbelievable array of masks, gowns and wigs were strewn in profusion about the long narrow room. Above her and to the left hung a macabre company of puppet figures which had been used in some long forgotten show. A grinning skull and a clown's face showed from the many masks.

Her head was reeling and she knew she was about to faint. And she began to wonder and worry about the coffee that Harry had brought her with her lunch. She had noticed at the time it had an odd taste, like almonds. Had she been given some drug? Was this the first step in their plan to make her mentally a cripple?

The room was now swirling and her grip on the door handle relaxed. Slowly she slumped down onto the rough wooden floor. Above her the army of grotesque masks peered down with an almost human quality of curiosity. She stared at the grinning, macabre cluster of faces until they were lost in a blur and she became unconscious.

Chapter Ten

There was a shrill of high-pitched laughter from above her. And she opened her eyes to a fantastic sight. Harry, the midget, was standing on the shelf above her where the masks were hanging.

"So you're coming to!" he said.

"Yes," she said weakly.

"How do you like my friends?" he demanded. And with another peal of mad laughter he began swinging the skull face at her and then the clown's exaggerated mask.

"Please, don't," she begged him.

"You shouldn't have come down here, you know," the midget warned her.

"I came by accident."

"You were trying to escape," he said curtly. "Don't bother to lie. And then you had one of your blackouts!"

"No," she said, sitting up and using the leg of one of the shelves to help rise to her feet. "No. It wasn't that. You gave me something in my coffee. I'm sure you did!"

"You're crazy!" the little man jeered at her.

"I know you put something in it," she insisted.

He nimbly made his way down from the shelf, using a chair as a ladder for part of the descent. Then he turned to her with an evil smile on his shrivelled face.

"You know what's happening to you," he said. "You're going crazy. Pretty soon you'll be as mad as Malenkov!" And he gave another shrill of laughter.

"Let me out of here," she said, starting toward the dressing room door.

"No," the midget snapped, getting between her and the door and covering her with the gun he whipped from his coat pocket. "You're so anxious to be down here — stay for awhile. Solon will be coming back. Maybe you should stay here until he comes!" And with that he backed away, opened the door, and vanished. The door closed and she heard a key turn in it.

After what seemed a very long while, Gale heard footsteps and a moment later someone unlocking the dressing room door. When it opened it was Jack who came in. His handsome face wore a look of annoyance.

"I hear you've been misbehaving," he said.

She was leaning against one of the shelves

weakly. "I suppose Harry told you that."

"Yes."

"That vicious little man lies about everything," she said.

He gave her a mocking look. "You mustn't be vindictive."

"He's horrid," she said.

"And you look wretched," Jack said with undisguised disgust. "Your dress is torn and stained and your hair is matted. Plus you don't have any make-up on."

"It's not the sort of place to make one want to look her best."

His lip curled. "You could do better. Solon thought you were looking ill. You must have a change of clothing and make-up with you."

"I haven't felt like bothering," she confessed. "When you decide you are faced with death or worse you don't worry too much about your appearance."

Jack lit himself a cigarette and took a deep puff on it. He studied her grimly as she stood there against the background of the costumes and masks.

At last, he said, "And I hear you've had another of your blackouts."

"No," she argued. "It wasn't anything like them. I'm sure Harry put something in my coffee. It was more like being drugged. I'm still not fully recovered from it yet."

"That's your imagination," he said.

"I don't think so."

"Why would Harry put drugs in your coffee?"

"To upset my mind," she said. "It's part of the doctor being here to see me."

"You have a sick imagination," he said, knocking the ash from his cigarette. "That's how you get those strange ideas."

She stared at him with sad disapproval. "How did I ever let you take me in as I did? Now I see you so clearly for what you are."

Jack remained unruffled. "You were delighted to have Mavis and me as your friends."

"I was a fool!"

"Not really," he said with a cold smile. "We played our parts extremely well. We've had a good deal of experience. Both of us knew just how to keep you interested."

"You should be proud. You did a fine job."

"There's a certain professional satisfaction," he agreed.

"What now?"

He eyed her in his cold way. "Solon will be back to talk to you again."

"I don't want to see him."

"You must."

"What about the ransom?" she asked.

"Your precious cousin is being slow about paying it."

"He's probably taking the police's advice," she said triumphantly. "I warned you he would."

"That won't do you any particular good," he replied confidently. "When Frank Solon starts a job he always carries it through."

"How did Solon know I was going to that particular summer resort?" she asked. "He had to, in order to send you there to trap me."

Jack's smile was overbearing. "That's a bit of information I can't pass on to you."

"It seems you can't give me any."

"Solon has it all worked out. Wait and see."

She said, "You can't leave me alone with Harry and Malenkov again. They're both more than a little mad."

He stubbed out his cigarette and ground it under his heel. "Mavis and I will be staying here for awhile."

This would make it even more difficult for her to escape from the old theatre. She said, "Where do you stay when you're here overnight?"

"We use a dressing room down here," he said. "This is directly under the stage. We can't all rate the star's room like you."

225

"You can have it anytime you like to change places with me," she told him bitterly.

The door opened wider and Mavis came in. The blonde gave Gale a look and said, "You're a nice mess. Your hair looks terrible."

"I've just been told that," she said. "And I don't care."

Mavis turned to her husband. "Harry says he wants her back upstairs."

"When I'm ready," Jack said in his arrogant way.

"I don't care what you do," his wife snapped. "I'm just delivering a message."

"It was Harry who locked her down here," Jack said. "He should have come back for her himself."

"You can settle that with him," Mavis said. And she went out in a sulk.

Jack watched after her a moment and then he told Gale, "You seem to always put her in a bad mood. I sometimes think she's jealous of you."

"That's funny under the circumstances," she said.

"Maybe. Women are crazy." He shrugged. "Harry says that you took the elevator down here in an attempt to escape."

"I came down to see what was here."

"If you've still got any ideas about getting

out of here let me put you straight," he continued. "All the windows at the basement and street level are both boarded and barred. The front entrance is boarded off and the only door by which you can get in or out is the cellar door we used when we came here. Have you got the picture?"

"It's not that complicated," she said. "And I suppose that one door is constantly guarded."

"That's it," Jack said. "So any escape ideas are silly. The upper exits are locked and most of the windows barred. Once you're in here you haven't a chance. That's why we can allow you as much freedom as we have. But we do like you to stay within the stage area."

"And I violated conditions by coming down here," she said acidly.

"Yes."

"I didn't make the conditions so I don't feel bound by them."

"Then put up with whatever unpleasantness Harry or Malenkov decide to dole out to you," the handsome man said. "Don't come to me for help or sympathy. You won't get it."

"I don't even expect it," she said.

"Now we'll go upstairs again," he told her. And they did.

Once again she was in the run-down suite which had in happier days been the star's dressing room. Harry brought her some dinner with a grin on his wizened little face and the promise that it was full of poison. He seemed to get great enjoyment from this pleasantry. Because she was hungry and doubted that he would so soon again place anything in her food she had some of the Chinese dinner. She was beginning to tire of chicken chow mein.

With dinner over she went to the dresser mirror and studied herself in its murky depths. Jack was right. Her hair was a mess and her face looked ominously pale. She brushed her hair a little and took some make-up and applied it to her pale cheeks. Lastly she switched from the soiled green linen she'd been wearing to a navy blue dress of the same style and material.

Freshening up made her feel a little better. Now she must wait through the evening and when night finally arrived make a real attempt to get away. She believed most of what Jack had told her about the impossibility of getting out of the old building. But she also felt that in a place as huge and ancient as the theatre there had to be some means of escape which had been overlooked.

It was up to her to find it. If she could get

her hands on one of the guns they all carried it would be an enormous help. Last night when Malenkov had sat slumped and asleep in the chair on the stage she might have been able to take his gun away from him. He must have had it in his lap to have used it so quickly. But she hadn't thought about it until it was too late.

From every angle Malenkov seemed her best hope of assistance. She had an idea he liked her in his confused way.

Thinking of him reminded her of the ghost, or whatever it was, that she'd encountered on the stage the previous night. The horror with the blotched face and hands bore no resemblance to the lovely Elena who Malenkov claimed moved about the old theatre in the small hours. The phantom female she'd seen had been a crone who reeked of the grave!

She wished she knew what the explanation was. In any attempts she made to get away from the old building that phantom figure could be a factor. Last night in her fearful reaction to the ghost she'd cried out and betrayed herself to her captors. What had happened once could conceivably happen again.

After a little she went out on the stage and there seemed to be no one around. She stared into the dark cave of the theatre auditorium and was awed by the silence that had suddenly enveloped the old building. She knew that Jack and Mavis preferred to spend much of their time in the office out front. And that is where they probably were now.

As for Malenkov and Harry they could be anywhere. With a sigh she strolled across the stage to the other side where the electrical board was situated. She scanned the big board recalling that some of the switches must be working since Harry had used the controls there to trap her on the revolving stage.

"Stop where you are," a weird cracking voice came from directly behind her.

She froze with fear. "Who is it?"

"No one you've ever seen." The eerie voice could belong to either a man or woman.

"What do you want?" she asked.

"To poison you," said the crazy voice, and suddenly there was a peal of shrill laughter.

She recognized Harry's laugh and turned around, her face crimson with shame that she had allowed him to make a fool of her again so easily with his ventriloquism. Of course he wasn't there and nowhere near her. She glanced around the stage in an effort to locate him.

"My you're stupid," a harsh male voice

exclaimed on her right.

"Where are you?" she demanded.

"Down here," came the reply in Harry's real voice and she looked down into the orchestra pit and saw his grinning, shrivelled face and also that Frank Solon was standing at his side looking amused. He had been putting on a show for the chief.

She stared down at the midget with annoyance. "You enjoy tormenting me, don't you?"

"About the only fun I get," Harry agreed.

Solon, still wearing his dark glasses in the shadowed theatre, turned to the little man and said, "You can go. I got things to tell her."

"Sure," Harry said. "She's all yours." And the little man scurried off up the aisle to the back of the theatre.

Frank Solon mounted the stairs leading from the orchestra pit to the stage and then he came over to face her. He said, "You look better."

"When am I to be allowed to leave?"

"There's no telling."

She frowned. "You said you had some news for me. Hasn't James Garvis paid you the ransom money?"

"No."

"I don't understand."

The Mafia chief's hawk face showed no expression. "Maybe he isn't so interested in getting you back."

"That's a lie," she cried.

He shrugged. "He's not doing anything about it."

"And he knows I've been kidnapped?"

"Yes."

She tried to decide whether Solon was telling the truth or not. She finally said, "If he hasn't paid you the ransom, it has to be because he has some other plan."

"Like what?"

"He must be working with the police."

"I doubt it."

"I don't," she said, gaining courage. "That's probably why he hasn't turned the money over to you. The police are likely closing in on you at this moment."

"You think so?"

"I do. It wouldn't be hard for them to guess that Jack and Mavis were the ones who kidnapped me. And I imagine they can be traced to you by one means or another. They've been working for you all along. And you were at the hotel yourself."

"Anyone can visit the hotel," he pointed out. "That doesn't mean I had anything to do with the kidnapping."

"They're bound to suspect you," she said

excitedly. "So now it's just a matter of finding this place. And they will."

He studied her in silence for a moment. "You've got it all figured out."

"I think so."

"You're nuts!"

She was taken back by his scorn. "Why?"

"Because I know more than you do."

"More about what?"

The dark glasses were fixed on her with cold arrogance. "I got news for you little Miss Rich. Your cousin isn't ever going to bail you out of here."

"Why do you say that?" She couldn't hide the fear in her voice. She had the feeling that whatever this man's character, he did not speak loosely.

"Because I know it," he said softly. "So it looks like you might not be going to live long."

"You daren't kill me!"

His face was scornful. "What gives you such a special right to life? Because you're young? Young people die and get killed every day. Because you're worth a fortune? That isn't going to help you here."

Her eyes widened. "Why do you hate me so?"

"Maybe because you're young and alive and healthy. You got everything to live for,"

233

Solon said in his cold, harsh fashion. "But you haven't earned any of it. You're just lucky that's all, Miss Gale Garvis. Suppose your luck has ended? Suppose the time has come for you to die?"

"What are you planning?" she whispered. "Why did you send that doctor here?"

"To make sure you were healthy," Solon said. "And you know what? He gave you a good report. What do you think about that? He thinks you're real healthy. Being a champion swimmer and all that stuff has given you a special body!"

"It doesn't matter now, does it?" she said dully.

"It matters more than you know," Frank Solon said. "Maybe I'll get some idea and your life needn't be wasted after all."

She couldn't believe the strange conversation was really taking place. "What do you mean?"

He smiled coldly. "I say life is a gift. Enjoy it while you have it."

"There's not much scope for enjoyment in here," she said bitterly.

"Sorry," he said.

"Why me?" she asked. "Why did you decide to kidnap me? There must be many other girls with wealthy parents. Why select me?"

"That's too long a story for now," he said in his harsh voice. "I'll be back to see you soon. Maybe I'll tell you then." With a curt nod he turned and walked back down the steps into the orchestra pit again. She watched as he went up the aisle to vanish in the darkness. Her mind was made up. As soon as midnight came she would make a fresh attempt to find a way out of the shabby old movie palace.

She went back to the star's dressing room and began the ordeal of waiting. At the same time she tried to make some sense out of what Frank Solon had said and she couldn't. Why hadn't James paid the ransom?

She started as a light knock sounded on her dressing room door. And then the door opened and Jack came in. He said, "How did you make out with Solon?"

"Not too well."

Jack sat on the arm of the easy chair. "He seemed in good enough humor. I figured you might have come to some arrangement."

She frowned. "I couldn't even understand what he was talking about most of the time."

"He can be like that," he admitted. "But he always knows what he's after."

"I gathered that."

Jack was studying her closely. "Do you hate me for getting you into this?"

She shrugged. "I think you're weak and despicable. Otherwise you'd not be Solon's henchman."

His cheeks flamed. "Solon would have found someone else to do the job if I hadn't taken it."

"You think so?" she taunted him.

"He pays well. There's always someone available," Jack said. "I've given you better treatment than you might have had."

"If he doesn't get the ransom money he'll kill me," she said. "I'm sure of it. Can I put that down to part of your kindness?"

His eyes became hard. "You might do better if you didn't keep nagging me," he warned her.

"I don't expect anything from you except possibly another betrayal," she said with scorn.

He got up from the chair. "Great. I'll try not to disappoint you."

"I'm sure you won't," she said quietly.

He went to the door and then turned to smile at her wryly. "I came here hoping I might be able to make things a little easier for you. Thanks for fixing it so I don't care." He left without waiting for her reply.

His words didn't bother her particularly. Solon had thoroughly frightened her and there was nothing that Jack could add to that.

The night wore on and no one else came to the shabby dressing room. A few minutes after midnight she opened the door and ventured out onto the stage. The chair which Malenkov had sat in the night before was vacant. There was no one in sight.

Emboldened, she walked to the edge of the stage and then made her way down the carpeted stairs leading to the orchestra level. When she reached it she pressed close to the wall and edged her way along toward the rear of the huge section.

Once again she was conscious of the glory the old theatre must have once known. The carpeting was still soft under her feet and though dust and even cobwebs covered the walls and light fixtures the fine architecture of the place could not be denied. The damp, stale odor of the closed theatre was strong in her nostrils and reinforced the word she'd been given that most of the windows had been boarded up.

Then there was a scurry of movement across the carpet and something squeaked and bumped past her feet. She had all she could do to restrain a scream. She knew it must have been a rat whose path had crossed hers in the dirt and darkness. She leaned close to the wall breathing heavily for an agonizing moment.

Far behind her on the stage the solitary night light offered its feeble glow. The main section of the theatre was in shadow. She could only see a short distance ahead. Now she resumed her slow progress toward the rear of the decaying old theatre. It seemed to be taking her hours but it could only have been a matter of minutes until she was in the entrance foyer.

She remembered its sad remnants of gilt grandeur from being briefly there the day she'd first been brought to the theatre as a prisoner. She crossed the foyer and tried to find the outer lobby leading to the street. When she reached the archway giving access to it she was stunned to find a solid wall had been built there. It seemed to partition the front area of the building for a shop or something of the kind.

Pressing her ear to the wall she listened for some sound on the other side but there was none. She was as badly off as before.

She knew that another of the archways led to the basement of the theatre and the door by which she'd come in. She'd been told by Jack there was always a guard at that door but she didn't know whether he'd told her the truth or not. There was only one way to find out and that was go down and see for herself.

It was easy to locate the stairs and in a few

moments she was crouching in the darkness of the damp cellar staring at the door leading to the outside. Once she managed to get through there she'd be certain of freedom. Her breathing quickened as she thought about this and looked for a guard. As far as she could tell there was none.

Gathering her courage, she started boldly across the cellar. She reached the inner door and quietly turned and opened it. Trembling with fresh hope she found herself in the cool vestibule between the door and the outer one at the top of a half-dozen concrete steps.

Escape was within easy reach. She had only to mount those stairs, open the other door and race down the alley outside and she'd be in a busy street where she could get help. Nerves on edge, she started up the steps and then her hand was on the knob of the outer door. She turned it and nothing happened. It was locked!

Despair crossed her pretty face. She tried the door again, putting her whole weight against it this time in an effort to force it open. It was a stupid act and a dangerous one. All at once an alarm sounded in the cellar. The clamor of the shrill bell cut through her and she knew she was in serious trouble.

Diving down the stairs she opened the

other door and went back inside. The noise of the alarm was deafening in there and she ran across the cellar to press herself close to the wall and wait breathlessly in the darkness.

"Down here!" she heard Harry shout. And a moment later he appeared with gun in hand.

She watched as the little man cautiously approached the door and checked to make sure there was no one there. Then he went to the outer door to find if it was locked. At the same time he must have touched some switch which shut off the alarm. He came back into the cellar looking like a puny child playing hide and seek in the shadows, except for the gun in his hand.

"What was it?" It was Jack, also with gun ready, who came down the stairs to join him.

"She must have reached here and tried the door," Harry said.

"Where is she now?" Jack asked, looking around, apparently not able to see her though she was clutching the wall not a dozen feet from him.

"The alarm must have sent her back into the theatre before we got here."

Jack still hesitated. "Would she have time?"

"Plenty," the midget said in an angry

tone. "I was below stage and I was the first one here. It took me several minutes."

"I was in the office. I thought Malenkov was watching the door," Jack said.

"He's supposed to be but you can't count on him. I've told Solon that," Harry said angrily. "I tell him, Malenkov is crazy. But he doesn't listen."

"She can't be anywhere here," Jack said. "We'd better make a search of the theatre."

The two men were still talking as they left the cellar and mounted the stairs to the foyer again. She remained motionless by the wall and hardly daring to breathe, not able to believe her luck.

After a while she went to the dark stairway and edged up to the top of it to listen. She could hear the sounds of their distant voices and those of Malenkov and Mavis as they all searched the theatre for her. Every so often they would call out. She had at least raised a storm of excitement in the dark old theatre.

She had an idea they were either in one of the upper balconies or in the area below the stage that was honeycombed with numerous dressing rooms and would take time to go through. She decided it was her chance to make her way down through the main section of the orchestra and reach the stage again. Once she'd made this decision she lost no time.

Within a few minutes she was on the stage and advancing toward her dressing room. Then she heard Harry's shrill little voice as he came up one of the stairways from below. Not wanting him to catch her out there she ran across the stage to hide in a dark corner.

She managed to reach it before he appeared, gun still in hand, and headed toward her dressing room door. He went inside and she took a deep breath as she debated her next move.

But before she could get her thoughts straight the decision was made for her. Emerging from the shadows and coming directly toward her was the ghost. She saw the blurred outline of the crone with the blotched face and outstretched claw-like hands and screamed. The frightening apparition with the straggly gray hair flowing around the horror of a face kept advancing so that she was now only a couple of feet away. A kind of weird groaning escaped the thing's lips.

Gale could stand it no longer. She screamed again and again and ran out onto the lighted portion of the stage. She saw Harry coming out of the dressing room alerted by her cries and found herself trapped in both directions. The only avenue of escape for her loomed straight in front of her. The ladder on the wall that led to the gallery hundreds of feet above. She ran to the ladder and began climbing up it.

As she went higher up the ladder she heard Harry down on the stage threatening her. He was making shrill, angry promises to shoot her if she didn't come down. But she paid no attention to him and kept climbing the narrow iron ladder which was attached to the wall.

Some of the others were now joining him and she heard their voices as if through a fog. It was taking all her energy and concentration to continue mounting the straight-up ladder. She was in the shadows of the gallery and breathless from her long exertions. But she dare not halt in her climb nor look down. A glance below might bring on dizziness or even one of her blackouts and send her crashing down to her death on the stage.

The voices crying out to her from the stage were like faint echoes as she reached the end of the ladder and the safety of the gallery loft. It was a platform about two-feet wide with a railing three-feet high and from it one could manipulate some of the intricate overhead scenic devices or get out on any one of the various catwalks that extended all the way across the roof of the stage.

The stage crew had used these narrow foot-wide walks with single light railings to venture out over the middle of the stage and straighten out any snarls in the scenery. Up here in the gallery the various painted drops were kept stored. And as a use came for them they were lowered into place. No one had been up there for years it seemed. Dust covered everything and her hands were thick with it.

She clung to the railing of the gallery loft and gazed down at the tiny figures at the bottom of the ladder far below. And now the full impact of the height struck her. She clung feverishly to the railing feeling she might pass out. But something caught her attention which steeled her nerves again. Jack had started to climb the puny iron ladder and was even now part way up to the gallery.

She stared down with horror as she saw Jack come grimly on up the ladder. In a few minutes he would be in the loft with her and take her in custody again. There was only one hope of escaping him, a move so dangerous that only sheer desperation drove her to it. She moved down the loft to the section where the first catwalk led out across the roof of the gallery. Holding her breath she dodged under the railing and transferred to the flimsy, narrow platform. As she stepped onto it and grasped its single guard rail she felt it quiver under her weight.

Chapter Eleven

For a sickening second she stood there frozen with fear, expecting to have the light platform collapse and send her hurtling down to her death. But after the initial swaying it seemed all right. As she moved along it, she was careful to keep one hand holding the railing. By the time Jack reached the loft platform she had gone far enough in the darkness of the gallery to be invisible to him.

But he'd know where she'd gone. In a moment he would himself venture out on one of the catwalks. And if he chose the right one he would eventually trap her at the far end of the fly gallery. The ladders went up on only one side.

Knowing this she moved on. She was in a world of shadows now, high above the dimly lighted stage. The motion of the platform no longer bothered her. She desperately hoped that Jack might lose his courage and not attempt to follow her out there. Then it would be a waiting game and when she was exhausted enough she could either drop to her death or meekly return to the loft and give herself up.

For the moment she held onto the railing and kept moving as far from the loft as she could get. She paused for breath and glanced toward the catwalks that ran parallel to the one she had chosen. They were separated from her by perhaps six feet. Too wide a distance to try to leap at such a dizzy height above the stage.

She was considering this when in the darkness of the walk on her left she all at once saw a shadowy figure. It came a little nearer her and took definite shape. She stifled a gasp as she recognized the thin, youthful face of Larry Grant! She couldn't decide whether it was wild fantasy on her part or she was really seeing him. He looked at her solemnly and placed a finger to his lips to warn her to silence. She stared at the shadowy figure on the other catwalk still not sure that it existed anywhere but in her troubled mind. And then Larry retreated into the darkness again and was lost to her.

Then she felt the catwalk sway and heard heavy breathing behind her. She turned to look into the angry, sweat-ridden face of Jack. He was only a yard or so away from her.

"You vixen!" he gasped angrily. "You've given me a fine fool's chase."

She leaned back against the flimsy railing. "Don't touch me!"

He halted within reach of her but didn't try to grasp her. "What made you do this crazy thing?"

"I had to get away from you! All of you!"

He glared at her. "Well, are you satisfied?"

"I won't leave here," she said. "Go back down."

Jack held onto the rail with one hand as he studied her grimly. "I'll give you two minutes to make up your mind. Either you come without a struggle or I'll take you back forcibly. And that could mean both of us ending up down there in a broken heap."

She knew that this time he was deadly serious. If she had really seen Larry, if Larry were truly hiding in the old theatre, then there might be hope for her. There was no need for her to struggle or end her life with a plunge downward at this point.

Jack said, "Well?"

"All right," she said quietly. "You go first. I'll follow."

He began moving back toward the loft a step at a time and she followed, keeping a distance between them. Their double weight on the catwalk was making it quiver ominously. Gale had visions of it giving way.

When they were within reaching distance

of the loft she told him, "You go first. Then you can help me."

He grasped the loft railing and lifted himself onto the platform. Then he held his hand out for her. "Ready?"

"Yes," she said weakly, grateful for the assistance of his hand as she made the return transfer to the solid loft.

When she was safely beside him, Jack gave her a scathing glance. "We still have to reach the stage."

She looked at the puny iron ladder which went straight down and closed her eyes. "I don't know whether I can!"

"You're like a frightened kitten at the top of a telephone pole," he said with disgust. "You've gotten up here and now you don't know how to get down."

"You go first!" she begged him.

"That won't help you," he said. "We'll have to try it together."

"How?"

"You get on the ladder and I'll get on at the same time, but I'll take the rung below you for my feet. At the same time I'll be able to keep my arm around you as we go down. You'll always be on the step directly above me. Do you understand?"

"I think so," she said in a thin voice. And then, "Why are you taking so much trouble?

If I'm to die anyway."

"You're my responsibility until Solon takes over," Jack said, his handsome face taut. "He wouldn't thank me for letting you fall down there."

"I don't understand you," she said, staring at him.

"You don't have to. Ready?"

She took a deep breath. "I suppose so."

"Go ahead," he told her. "I'll be right with you."

And thus they began their slow descent of the narrow ladder. In their favor was the fact that the ladder was firmly imbedded in the concrete wall. It offered no motion of any sort and so they had only to cling to it and to each other.

Part way down she began to get a painful cramp in her right hand. "My hand is going bad," she quavered. "I don't think I can hold on with it!"

"Open and close it a few times," he ordered her.

"It's killing me!" she sobbed.

"Keep on using it," was his firm command.

And so she did. And after a moment of crisis it became less painful and she was able to get a kind of grip with it. On the last twenty feet of their descent she could vaguely hear the voices of the others waiting on the stage.

Then her feet touched the ground and she was looking into the wrinkled, evil face of the midget. Harry was studying her with a mixture of hatred and disgust.

"I didn't think you'd be that crazy," he shrilled at her.

The ancient Malenkov shook his head. "At any moment you could have fallen."

"She wanted to be rescued by Jack," Mavis said with a sneer on her hard face.

"There wasn't anything certain about that either," Jack said with a deep sigh.

"What made you go up there?" Harry demanded. "I saw you start and tried to stop you."

She felt the time had come to tell them. "I saw the ghost."

Malenkov gasped. "The ghost! You saw Elena!"

"No," she said. "It wasn't Elena. At least not as you described her to me. This phantom was old and horrible. Like a dreadful witch. She came toward me. I was terrified and made for the ladder."

Harry was staring at her with disbelief. "I didn't see any ghost!"

Gale pointed to the rear of the stage. "She was there in the dark."

Jack was frowning. He asked Gale, "Is this on the level?"

"Why should I lie about it?"

"Because you tried to escape and had us running all over the place in a frenzy. This sounds like a story to try and confuse us."

"All right," she said. "Believe that if you want to."

"I'm interested in the truth," Jack said.

"You won't get it from her," Mavis snapped. "I say it's time to forget this and all return to our beds." She was wearing a fancy dressing gown over a night dress.

"Maybe you're right," Jack said. He nodded to Gale. "Come on." And he escorted her back to the door of her dressing room. "Do I have to lock you in for the rest of the night or have you learned your lesson?"

She sighed. "I know I can't get away."

"Then don't try any more fool stunts," he warned her. "Otherwise it's lock and key for you from now on."

"There's no need."

"Harry will be posted on the stage for the night," Jack told her. "So you may as well relax."

She went inside with his derisive comment ringing in her ears. She was exhausted and her nerves were shattered. But out of the failure and devastating experience there had come one faint ray of hope. She was sure she'd seen Larry Grant up there on the other catwalk. It had been so real she couldn't put it down to imagination. And if Larry was in the theatre it meant that he had come to help her.

She was too excited to sleep. She lay there with the blankets over her thinking about it all. As a further precaution she'd left the light on in the dressing room; it gave her a feeling of security which she badly needed at this moment.

It seemed certain she could never escape from the kidnappers on her own. So she needed a Larry to come to her assistance. Jack had surprised her with his grim show of courage. She felt it had been the pressure of knowing how angry Solon would be if she were killed in a fall that had pushed him on.

Yet Frank Solon had made it fairly plain that he intended she should die. Why should it make a difference how she died? Probably because it would be considered a breach of his authority. Her death was to take place at his command, and only then.

It was all madness. And she was caught up in the midst of the whirlpool. Her thoughts returned to James Garvis. It struck her that her cousin was taking a great gamble in refusing to pay the ransom. How could he risk her life that way even though he was against the principle of paying off her kidnappers? Better to rescue her and worry about the ethics later.

Very gradually she became sleepy. Her eyes drooped shut and she was soon in the midst of a nightmare in which her father, Rufe and Emily all played parts. Emily was alive again and so was her father. She was talking with them in the garden when Rufe came to join them, his face angry. He began making loud accusations against Emily. Her father stepped in between the lanky long-haired youth and Emily and at the same instant Rufe produced a gun and shot him. Then he turned and shot Emily as well.

As the bodies of the two crumpled on the gravel of the garden path she backed away screaming. Rufe gave her a frightened look and dropped the gun. In the next instant he was racing from the scene of the crime. She knelt by the body of Emily and saw the blood staining her dress and the ground around her. It was a signal for her to black out.

She was running in a forest filled with a strange fog. And Jack was pursuing her. She had no idea where she was or where she might be going. She only knew that Jack intended to kill her and she somehow must escape him. The ground was rough and uneven and the forest seemed to be in a swamp.

Seeing a space between trees she left the path and dodged into what she hoped might be a sanctuary. She pushed her way through the bushes with the thick mist rising up to veil everything. Suddenly she had lost firm ground and was sinking down into a mire of quicksand. She struggled to save herself to no avail. The more she fought to escape from the greedy slime the more completely did she become its victim. Now she was in the mud to her armpits.

She cried out to be rescued. And from the mists there appeared the midget, Harry. He stood there looking at her with an evil smile on his wrinkled old-man's face.

"Don't move or cry out," the midget told her.

Gale opened her eyes wide in despair and found herself looking up at Larry Grant. And he was telling her, "Quiet!"

Aware that her nightmare had faded and this was reality, she whispered, "I was dreaming. I thought I saw you in the gallery. But I couldn't believe it."

"I was there," he whispered in return.

"How did you know?"

"I'll tell you that later," he said.

"They mean to kill me."

"Not yet," he assured her. "They're not

ready yet. I wanted to let you know."

"What does it all mean?" she asked.

"Complicated," he said, his thin face concerned. "I'd like to get you out of here tonight but I can't."

"Why?"

"A lot of reasons," he sighed. "Just hold on and try to keep from panicking."

"I tried to find a way out," she said despairingly. "I just can't manage it alone."

He nodded. "I know."

Her eyes searched him worriedly. "Are you one of them, too?"

"No." But he didn't make it sound convincing.

"Then how did you manage to get in the theatre and here to talk to me?"

"I can't tell you that either," the young man said. "All I ask is that you have faith in me."

"Can you get a message to my cousin? To the police?"

"I'll try," he said. "I'm going now. Believe that I'll be back and you'll be saved."

He bent close and kissed her. And the next instant he turned and hurried to the door leading to the stage. He opened it a crack, took a careful look outside, and then went on out. She watched with baffled eyes as he shut the door softly after him. There had been so many things she'd wanted to question him about and hadn't had time.

The ghost for one. And his relationship to the gang for another. She now began to feel convinced that Larry must be in with them. It was the only explanation of his being in the theatre. So even his friendship had been a tarnished one. It saddened her to realize she'd been tricked by them all.

If Larry Grant did decide to help her it would only be because he turned his back on Solon and the others. And his motive for doing that might only be that he was afraid the gang had gotten themselves in too dangerous a spot. He could save himself by turning her protector.

And she'd been wondering if she weren't in love with him! This knowledge depressed her. Even if he should rescue her she would never be certain whether it was to escape conviction himself or because he loved her.

Finally she slept again. But it was a nightmare-filled sleep and when she awoke in the morning she felt as weary as when she'd gone to bed. It was Malenkov who brought her breakfast rather than the midget.

"Harry had to go somewhere for the boss," was the old organist's explanations as he put the tray down.

She looked at the scarecrow figure of what

had once been a talented musician. And she said, "I'm glad you came. It gives us a chance to talk."

His sunken eyes regarded her with uneasiness. "I don't want to get in any trouble," he said.

"You're the only one among them with any feeling," she insisted.

Brightening, he glanced toward the door to be sure it was closed and they wouldn't be overheard. Then he came near her and in a low confidential tone said, "You're right! I'm not like them. They call me crazy but I'm better than all of them!"

"I know you are," she encouraged him.

Malenkov looked at her eagerly. "You saw the ghost last night?"

"I saw a ghost," she corrected him. "But it wasn't a beautiful ghost like your Elena."

"Tell me about it," he urged her, his body crouched.

"The ghost I saw was old and ugly. She had a blotched face and thin awful hands. There was a stench of death about her and her clothing was dust-covered as if she'd just emerged from her coffin."

The bald man listened intently. "It sounds like Flora Foster."

The name was new to her. "Flora Foster?"

"She was the featured singer here for

258

years. She did a solo every show. And after the place did away with stage presentations she married. No one saw her for ages. She came back here about eighteen months ago. She was old, bloated and an alcoholic. She was broke and begged to be allowed to stay here in the theatre with Harry and me."

"And you didn't let her?"

"No. I wanted to but Harry said no. He was already mixed up with Solon then and knew what we'd be using the theatre for. He said Solon wouldn't allow any crazy alcoholics coming in and out. So he sent her away."

"And?"

"About a month later she was run down by a car. She was drunk at the time and she was wandering around late at night. She died in the hospital."

The eccentric old man's description of Flora Foster sent a chill of fear through her. It so fitted the appearance of the specter she'd seen.

"And I can see why she'd come back to this place," he went on. "She loved this theatre. Probably knew her happiest days here."

"The figure I saw was horrible."

"She looked bad the last time I talked with her," Malenkov agreed. "You'd never guess that she had once been beautiful and with a voice that really counted."

"So more than one ghost haunts this place," she said, staring at the grimy walls of the dressing room.

"It's filled with ghosts of the past," Malenkov said, a look of awe on his emaciated face. "Sometimes I can hear them whispering. And when I play, Elena comes to the gallery and stands by the organ."

She hated to take advantage of the mad old man yet she knew she needed his help, so she forced herself to say, "Do you think your Elena would approve of what you're doing now? Would she want to have you working with that Harry, the one who caused her death?"

The old man in the tattered clothes looked uneasy. He waved her argument aside with a grimy hand. "That was long ago. Things are different now. I have to go along with that midget. Else he'd tell Solon and I'd lose my job. Then I'd be worse off than Flora Foster was!"

"So you haven't the courage to do what you believe is right?"

"I'm an old man," he whined. "If I were parted from my music I'd have nothing left to live for."

"If you'd help me get free of here I'd see

you were well taken care of for the rest of your life," she told him. "And I'd make sure you had an organ to play."

Malenkov showed alarm. He glanced toward the door again and then bent close to her. "You shouldn't say such things to me. It could get us both in a lot of trouble."

"I have nothing to lose. They mean to kill me."

He shook his head. "It's no use. I would if I dared. But I'd never survive if I left here. And no other organ would be the same to me as the one up in that loft. I have to stay here where Elena's spirit is."

"They'll tear the theatre down one day soon," she warned him. "Then what will you have left?"

"Don't talk about it," he begged her.

She felt she had pursued the point long enough. Better now to give him time to think about it on his own. She said, "Turn it over in your mind. In the meantime there is something you may be able to tell me."

"What?"

"Is there anyone by the name of Larry working for Solon?"

"Larry?" he repeated the name blankly.

"Yes."

"Could be. He has so many that come and go. I lose track of them."

She said, "He's young and he has red hair and a rather lean face."

The old man considered. "I don't know for sure."

"I'd expect you to remember him because of his hair," she said. "It's a rust red."

The mad organist looked uneasy. "I don't take much notice of people. That's the way I am. I think I've seen him. I can't be sure."

As he finished speaking the door opened and Jack came in. He gave them both sharp glances. Then he told Malenkov, "You've been here a long time."

"We were talking," she said, quickly.

Jack eyed her coldly. "I guessed that." To Malenkov he said, "What were you talking about?"

The old man seemed stricken with fear. "We were talking about the theatre and my playing the organ."

"That doesn't sound very interesting to me," Jack observed acidly.

Gale came forward to the two men. "He's telling the truth. I was asking him questions about the theatre in the old days."

Jack's face was grim. "You're both very glib about it. How do I know you weren't trying to get him to help you escape?"

"I wouldn't do that!" Malenkov exclaimed nervously.

Jack's face was angry. "I wouldn't expect you to be fool enough to admit it if you did consider it," he said.

"Don't blame him for my talking too much," she said.

"Let me warn both of you there's no way out of this place without Solon's permission," Jack said.

"Sure, Jack," Malenkov said humbly. "I'm sorry I stayed so long in here. I meant no harm."

"He knows that," Gale said by way of comforting the old man. "He's just trying to scare me. Please go and when you get a chance play some of your music for me. I like to hear you."

Malenkov nodded. "Yes, I'll do that. I'll be glad to!" And he hurried out of the dressing room.

Jack stared at her. "I thought you learned your lesson last night."

"What do you mean?"

"There's no escape. And trying to talk that madman into helping you won't get you anywhere."

She looked at him defiantly. "How can you be so certain that is what I was doing?"

"I could sense it the moment I stepped in here," he said scornfully. "You both looked guilty."

"The way you came in glowering at us that could be expected," she told him.

He smiled sourly. "You can play a part well. I give you credit for that."

"Not as well as you or Mavis. Otherwise I wouldn't be here," she said.

"You can't forgive us, can you?"

"Never."

"Well, you're fixing us up with enough trouble," he said. "I wish Solon would get on with things and end this."

She looked at him very directly and said, "My kidnapping is no ordinary one, is it?"

"What do you mean?" he asked, looking startled.

"Just what I said. What's the mystery? There's more to my being kept a prisoner here than Solon collecting ransom money."

He was silent for a moment. "What makes you think that?"

"Everything that has happened since I've been here. I wish I could fit it all together. Where does the doctor and his examination of me come into it, for example?"

"Nothing wrong in our wanting to keep you healthy," he said with a nasty smile. "You'll be all right if you just get the idea of escaping out of your head."

"I can't make any promises," she said.

"You'd be wise to," was his advice. "I'm

not going to lock you up. Not yet anyway. But after I tell Solon about the trick you played last night he may order me to."

He left her to have her breakfast. Her nerves were still in a bad state. And now she had the added worry that Jack might decide to remove Malenkov from the building so there'd be no danger of his attempting to help her. She knew that Jack believed they'd been going over the possibility of her escaping.

She was also still troubled by the belief that Larry Grant was one of the group who had kidnapped her, even though the old organist hadn't been able to confirm her fears. It wouldn't be possible for Larry to have access to the theatre as he had if he weren't in with them.

By now she had given up all hope of James paying the ransom. She was even beginning to doubt that a ransom note had reached him. It might be that she'd been kidnapped for some other reason of which she was not yet aware. She couldn't imagine what it might be. But the doctor's visit and all the veiled talk made her extremely suspicious.

The day dragged by without event. She left her room to wander about the stage but either Mavis or Jack always seemed to be around. She was sure they were watching her more closely . . . and Malenkov had suddenly vanished. She hadn't seen a sign of him since he'd left her room after delivering breakfast. She began to worry that Jack might have harmed him in some way.

She even inquired about him. "Where's Malenkov?" she asked Jack as they met on the stage.

"Why are you so concerned about him?"

"I've missed him. He hasn't been around all day," she told him.

Jack seemed pleased at her anxiety. He said, "He's been out on an errand. And so has Harry."

"I wondered if you were abusing him because of his friendship toward me," she said bitterly.

"I wouldn't think of it," Jack said mockingly.

She walked away from him to the other side of the wide stage. Glancing back to the dark shadowed area she recalled the ghost that had stalked her the previous night — Flora Foster, according to Malenkov.

She was standing there thinking of the phantom and all the other ghosts that inhabited the old theatre when she was jolted from her reverie by the sound of the organ playing. She glanced up at the first great roar from the organ and saw that Malenkov was in the loft bending over the keys of the beloved instrument.

The organ sounded out with more majesty and fury than ever before. And she felt some of it was for her. She'd praised his playing and he was giving her a special demonstration. But the music was really too loud. It fairly blasted through the empty theatre.

In the midst of it all the meticulously dressed Frank Solon stepped up onto the stage. The Mafia chief turned his attention upward, the dark glasses still the prominent feature of his hawk face. She saw the rage shadowing his swarthy features and felt worried for Malenkov.

"Stop!" the Mafia chief shouted.

But the man in the organ loft was lost in his playing. Solon shouted his order again but his voice was drowned by the volume of the organ music. Gale watched the drama in fascination: the gangster shaking with anger in the center of the stage, his orders had been ignored and the old madman blissfully swaying over the keys of the organ.

Jack came scurrying across the stage to Frank Solon, strain showing on his handsome face. "I didn't hear you arrive," he said.

Solon glared at him. "No wonder! With this going on!"

"He just started a while ago," Jack said.

"I want it stopped," Solon screamed. "Where are the wires leading to the loft?"

"Over by the elevator," Jack said, staring at him.

"Rip them out," Solon shouted. "Remove the fuses! I don't care what you do! But stop that noise!"

Jack didn't wait. He left the stage to go over to the array of fuse boxes along the wall. Eventually he found the ones controlling the power going to the organ and switched them off. The silence came with shocking impact. It filled the empty theatre just as the barrage of music had. There was a cry of frustration from the organ loft.

"You, up there!" Frank Solon shouted, raising his face to the organ loft again.

Malenkov came to the rail. "What is wrong? What has happened to the organ?"

"I've had it turned off," the Mafia chief said. "And I intend to keep it off."

"You can't!" Malenkov protested and vanished from the rail.

Frank Solon turned to Jack and told him, "I want you to make sure that organ is cut off from power permanently."

"The old man will be upset," Jack warned him.

"You heard me," the Mafia chief said grimly.

At the same instant Malenkov came out of the elevator door and ran across the stage to Solon. "What have you done?"

"Finished that organ for good," the hawk-eyed man snarled at him.

The old organist stared at the Mafia chief and a strange look came into his sunken eyes. A look that told Gale she now had someone she could count on for help.

Chapter Twelve

Now Frank Solon turned to her and said, "I want to talk to you alone. Go on inside."

She moved across the stage to the door of the dressing room as Malenkov still stood there looking stunned. Jack was with him and showing some strain because of the angry scene which had just taken place. She was followed by the Mafia chief and when they entered the shabby room which had been hers since she'd been held captive he shut the door.

Quite calm and collected again the man in the jaunty gray straw hat, neat gray flannel suit and dark glasses faced her. He said, "You'll be leaving here tomorrow night."

The unexpected announcement raised her hopes. "My cousin has paid the ransom money?"

"You'll know about that later," the cold Solon said.

"Why can't I go right away?" she asked.

"Because that doesn't suit me."

"I see," she said, her initial hopes beginning to fade slightly.

"You can pack your stuff for around ten. You'll be leaving here late."

"Where are you taking me?"

"You'll find that out tomorrow night," Solon told her. "I hear you tried to get away. That wasn't smart."

"It was normal," she retorted.

"Well, don't do anything to mess things up at this point. You'll be gone from here in twenty-four hours."

She had the worrisome feeling that the move he was talking about wasn't destined to make her all that happy. "I'd feel better about it if I knew where I was going."

"I thought you just wanted out of here."

"I want my freedom!"

"That will follow," he said.

"I hope so," she told him. "But I don't think I believe you."

She could feel the power of the malevolent eyes behind those dark glasses. He said, "You've never had a very high opinion of me."

"That's true."

"You think I'm some kind of monster," he said harshly. "But I happen to be a good husband and father. What do you think of that?"

"I'm not impressed," she said.

His smile was menacing. "Suppose I'm

able to prove it to you?"

"I'm sure you can't."

"Give me time," he said. "I've even got you lined up for a good deed. In spite of you, I'm going to make your useless life worth something."

She stared at him. "Now you're talking in riddles again. I think you're as mad as Harry or Malenkov in your own way."

"Maybe I am," he said. "We'll see about that. Just you be ready tomorrow night like I said."

Having delivered this message again he went on out. Alone in the murky light of the ancient dressing room she stood there staring after him for a long moment. All that he had said pointed to some immediate and serious development in the kidnapping scheme. Had James paid him off or had something gone wrong which made it necessary for her to be moved to another hiding place?

And what had the references to his family meant? Why had he brought up the subject of being a good husband and father? And what had he been going on about when he'd talked of forcing her to do a good deed? It was all so baffling. Yet one fact remained outstandingly clear, Solon was an evil character, no matter what he pretended.

The door opened and Mavis came in,

looking pleased with herself. "You've heard the word?"

"About my leaving?"

"Yes."

"Solon just told me."

Mavis lifted her eyebrows. "I'd expect you to be pleased. You don't look very happy."

"I'm not. I'm sure there's something behind it."

"Why?"

"None of you would be so relaxed if there weren't. You don't dare set me free after all I've found out. You can't risk my indicting you."

Mavis brushed the ash from her cigarette with a little finger and gave her a twisted smile. "You're getting sharper. If you'd been on your toes this way when we met at the resort you wouldn't be a prisoner here now."

"I was an innocent then, wasn't I?" Gale said disconsolately.

"The easiest mark I ever handled," Mavis bragged. "But then you had a crush on Jack. That helped."

"You're wrong," she said. "I was an easy victim for you because I was lonely and ill. My sister had just been murdered."

"And you had those blackouts," Mavis recalled. "You don't seem to be bothered so much with them here."

"Maybe having to be strong has been good for me," she said.

"Sure. Thank us for bringing out the best in you," Mavis said with a mocking laugh.

"I guess I should," she said quietly. It was, strangely enough, the truth. She had become more independent and resourceful. And her last blackout had been a minor one and was fairly far behind her. She would have liked to question the blonde about Larry and his part in the kidnap plot but she didn't want to give her the pleasure of taunting her.

"What's this talk about your seeing a ghost?" Mavis asked.

"Who told you that?"

"That crazy Malenkov has been mumbling about it. You know he thinks some old girl friend of his haunts this place."

"I have seen something," she said, sensing a mood of fear under the blonde's hard facade.

"Malenkov claims the ghost knocks on Harry's dressing room door every night because the midget killed her."

"Perhaps it's true."

Mavis looked unhappy. "I've never seen any ghost. And Malenkov is touched in the head. At least we'll not have to listen to his wild playing on the organ again."

"That wasn't very kind of Solon," she said.

"Solon doesn't deal in kindness," the blonde informed her. "You needn't expect any either."

"I don't," she said.

Mavis lingered a few minutes longer, almost as if she wanted to ask more questions about the ghost, but she apparently changed her mind and left rather abruptly in the end.

Gale went to bed. And once again her sleep was plagued by terrifying dreams. She woke with a start long after midnight to stare into the darkness of the dressing room and see a shadowed figure standing close to the door.

"Who's there?" she demanded, raising on an elbow, her flesh raising from fear.

There was no reply, just a faint rustling in the shadows. And then the figure moved closer and she was able to see it more clearly. It was the phantom figure of the ancient Flora Foster. The blotched face of the one-time star of the theatre showed a look of pain and sorrow. She stretched out a hand and made that same moaning sound again.

"No!" Gale screamed for her to go away.

The horrible looking old creature hesitated briefly and then turned and vanished somewhere in the darkness. She'd no sooner disappeared than the door of the dressing room was flung open and Harry entered with a flashlight in his hand.

He beamed the flashlight on Gale and asked, "Why did you yell out?"

"The ghost!"

The midget switched on the overhead light so she could see his diminutive form draped in a dressing gown. His evil, wrinkled face had taken on a look of fear.

"What ghost?" he demanded in his shrill voice.

"The one I've seen before," she said, still shaken by the eerie experience.

"There are no ghosts here," he snapped, but he still looked uneasy.

"What about the one who knocks on your dressing room door?" she said, watching to see his reaction.

It was prompt. He looked shocked. "What did you say?"

"You know," she said quietly.

The midget bit his lip as he glowered at her. "You mind your own business," he said. "Keep your light on for the night. It'll be your last one here." And he went out and slammed the door.

Her mention of the ghost had obviously bothered him. There must be some truth in

Malenkov's story that the long-dead Elena came to his door each night and tapped on it with ghostly fingers.

Somehow she got through the night and the following day. But she sensed a new tension in all the others with her in the ancient movie palace. Harry was very much in evidence and Malenkov sat moping on a bench on the stage most of the time. She waited until she had a chance to talk to him alone and then went and sat with him.

"I'm sorry about what they did to the organ," she sympathized with him.

The grimy old man turned his sunken eyes on her. "Thank you," he said quietly.

"There was no need for Solon to do that."

The mad organist's eyes showed an angry light. "Solon is a monster," he said. "Now I have nothing! Nothing at all!"

"At least you're still in the theatre," she said. "He hasn't tried to drive you out of here."

"He'll try that next," Malenkov predicted. "As soon as he finds someone to take my place. He needs a cover-up for what he's doing here."

She sighed and glanced out at the gaping darkness of the abandoned auditorium. "It will only be a matter of time before the whole theatre is torn down."

Malenkov sadly joined her in studying the silent old theatre. "I should have left long ago. I can still play. I could have found a place somewhere. But I stayed on and let my madness conquer me."

"It's not too late yet," she said.

"It is for me." He gave her a worried glance. "You'd better not sit here any longer. If they see us together they'll be making more accusations."

"You're right," she said. And she hastily got up and went back to the dressing room.

Harry came with her dinner a little while later. "Chinese food," he told her with a malicious wink. "You've had enough of it lately to get to like it."

"It's better than the surroundings," she told him.

"You'll be changing them in a couple of hours," he said. "Don't forget to pack and be ready when Solon comes."

She paid no attention to him. Her only opportunity to show rebellion was to ignore his order. And so when she'd finished the meal she began to pace nervously up and down. She was doing this when Jack came into the room.

"Are you packed?" he asked.

"No," she said, halting before him.

The handsome man looked bleak. "Solon

278

will soon be here and he expects you to be ready."

"Then he's in for a disappointment," she said. "I'm in no hurry to leave until I know where I'm going."

"He'll tell you when he comes," Jack said.

"You know now," she accused him. "Why don't you tell me?"

"Because it will come better from him."

She studied him scornfully. "You're afraid to tell me, aren't you?"

He hunched uneasily before answering and then said, "Why do you say that?"

"I can tell! It has something to do with that doctor and the examination, hasn't it?"

"Maybe."

"What horrible thing is Solon planning to do to me?" she asked with real anguish.

"I can answer that best myself." It was Solon who said this in his harsh way as he stood framed in the door opening.

Startled, she turned her attention to him. "I'm waiting to hear," she said in a taut voice.

He mentioned to Jack to leave the dressing room. "I can manage this better alone," he said.

"Sure," Jack said. "If you want me I'll be outside."

Solon waited until he went out, then told

her, "You'd better sit down."

"Will it take that long?"

"Who knows?" Solon said. "Take a chair anyway."

She sat in a plain chair and stared at him expectantly. "Well?"

"You're still out to give trouble," he said. "You've got your head filled with a lot of crazy ideas. But you've never guessed the true reason why you're here."

"I'll admit that," she said quietly.

He began to pace slowly before her. "You'll be leaving here in an hour or so."

"And it's useless to ask where you're taking me."

He swung around facing her. "Not anymore. I'm taking you away from here in a car. A car with a specially trained driver."

She frowned. "Why a specially trained driver?"

The Mafia chief's face was grim. "Let me start at the beginning. You were never kidnapped for ransom in the first place. I got you as part of a deal."

She couldn't believe her ears. "Part of a deal?"

"Sure," he jeered at her. "If this had been a regular kidnap deal you'd have been out of here long ago."

"Then what are you holding me for?" she

asked, the memory of the doctor uppermost in her mind and the old fears rising high in her.

"I needed a healthy young girl like you."

"What for?" she asked sharply.

He smiled at her coldly. "For no reason you might be thinking," he said. "I've said before I'm a good family man."

"So?"

"I have a daughter, just about your age," he said. "And for months now she's been hanging between life and death. She's a very sick girl. And the doctors tell me if a miracle doesn't happen she's going to die. And soon!"

"I'm sorry," she said. "But what does that have to do with me?"

He eyed her in silence for a long moment. Then he said dryly, "You're my miracle."

"I am?" she asked in astonishment.

He nodded. "My daughter has a bum heart. Bad leak and all that stuff. It can't be fixed. But with the proper donor she could have a heart transplant and maybe make it. At least for a year or two. And right now that's enough for me."

Gale got to her feet. "You're insane!" she said. "You're telling me you want my heart for your sick daughter!"

"That's it," he agreed. "And I'm going to have it."

"How? I'm still alive!"

"Not for long," he said coolly.

"You have to be crazy!" she gasped. "If you murder me you'll gain nothing. No reputable doctor would be involved in it."

"No doctor will have to know," he said.

"But how?"

"You're going to have a car accident," he told her very calmly. "That's why you're leaving here with a special driver."

"A car accident!" she gasped.

"Right," the Mafia chief said. "The man driving is trained for this kind of business. He'll manage the crash and if you're not smashed up bad enough he'll arrange that too."

"It's too fantastic!"

"We've done it before for other reasons," the man in the dark glasses assured her. "This guy has experience. Take a dark country road, the right kind of wash-out, car goes off the road by accident and it's maybe a half-hour before the police get there."

"It couldn't work," she protested. "They'll know I was kidnapped, that there's something wrong."

Solon gave her a cold smile. "You've never been reported as kidnapped."

"What?"

"You heard me."

"But my cousin James was expecting me. He'd be bound to contact the police. They have to be searching for me!"

"They aren't," he assured her.

"Why not?" she cried, frustrated to the point of near hysteria.

"Because you phoned him and told him you were running away with a new boy friend you met at that resort."

"I what?"

"We fixed all that. You've been driving around the country for all these days and nights with a hippie you picked up."

"No!" She could feel the darkness closing in around her.

He laughed. "It works out, see? When the accident happens the hippie goes into a panic and runs away. Another driver comes by and sees the car wrecked in the ditch and phones the police."

"No!" she sobbed, her hands pressed to her mouth.

He came close and took her by the hands. "Yes. And then you get shipped to the hospital and within a few hours your good healthy heart will be going into my Gina's body!"

"You're mad!"

"Consider yourself lucky," he said, his grip on her arms so tight it hurt. "I could just kill you and toss you in a field somewhere to rot. This way your body is going to be of some use. You're going to help someone live."

She stared at him through tear-dimmed eyes. "That's what you meant when you told me you were going to make me useful in spite of myself!"

"That's it!"

Suddenly she had an idea. "It won't work," she said. "You can't do that operation without my cousin's permission. And James will be suspicious. He'll never give it."

Solon smiled craftily. "He's already given it."

She was stunned. "How? What trick have you used?"

"You're slow catching on," the Mafia head said. "You've been wondering how I knew where you were going for a holiday. I'll tell you. Your cousin James fingered you for me."

"He what?"

"He put you on the spot," the man with the dark glasses said harshly. "He told me where you would be and when, so I could send those two after you."

"James wouldn't!"

"You are an innocent," he jeered. "James hired one of my people to murder your sister."

"Oh, no!" The enormity of it was beyond her. "You're telling me that James had Emily killed?"

"He did. And that put him in debt to me. And he promised to pay the debt by turning you over to me."

"Knowing I'd be murdered as well?"

"Sure. That way he's left to collect the estate. He wanted both you girls out of the way."

She listened in a dazed fashion. "So there wasn't any real kidnapping! James never was asked to pay ransom! It was to end this way from the start!"

He let go her wrists. "You've got it."

"I have no one," she said in a small voice. "No one."

"Your cousin sold you out," he jeered. "But you're going to do one last good deed. Save my Gina."

She stared at him with anguished eyes. "I'm sorry for you," she said.

"Sorry for me?" He sounded surprised.

"You think you're some kind of a god. That you can manage anything. Give your daughter life. For all your evil power you're bound to fail."

He regarded her derisively. "No," he said, "I'm not. Pack your stuff. You'll be leaving in the car in a quarter hour." And with this demand he left her.

She sank into the chair again and held her head in her hands. James was the evil genius behind it all! She could have guessed earlier. Right after Emily had been killed and he'd thrown all the suspicion on Rufe! Poor Rufe!

And now she was to be conveniently erased. But Solon would have her heart. It was a macabre thought. To know that within a few hours she would cease to exist as a person but her heart would live on in the body of Solon's daughter. She would still be a prisoner of his evil.

And there was nothing she could do. Within minutes she'd be whisked away from the old theatre on the first portion of the journey which would end in her death. James would pretend to be crushed at the news of her accident and donate her heart for the transplant.

A creaking sound from behind her caught her attention. And she turned in mixed fear and surprise to see a panel opening in the rear wall of the dressing room and the crouched figure of Malenkov emerging.

The old man warned her to be silent and motioned for her to join him. Without hesitation she crossed the room and entered the door to the secret passage. He at once closed the door and they were left standing in darkness in a narrow passageway.

The old organist whispered, "I had to come to you. I know what they're planning."

"Can we get out?" she whispered in return.

"I think so," he said. "It won't be easy."

"How?"

"This passage opens out onto the stage near the elevator door to my organ loft," he said. "I've known about it for years. If we can dodge across to the elevator there's another doorway leading to the second balcony. Once we get there I know a way out."

He started along in the darkness and she clung to his arm. In a few seconds they had come to the secret door opening onto the stage. Malenkov peered out a crack of the door and then signalled her urgently. They both emerged on the stage and raced across to the elevator door. No one was in sight and they managed the safety of the elevator without any difficulty. Malenkov gave her a triumphant glance as he pressed the button to send the elevator up to the loft.

"I had to think it all out," he told her. "I knew this was the only way."

The elevator came to a halt and they left it to enter the organ loft. Malenkov at once led her to another door painted the same gray as the wall. She'd never noticed it before.

"Emergency exit to the second balcony in case the elevator stopped working," he explained as he opened the door.

She saw a narrow, dark flight of steps and followed him up them. The steps were steep and twisted at the top to eventually give way to another door. Malenkov opened it and they were in a balcony box.

"We have to go across the balcony," he warned her in a whisper.

She nodded and followed him. They were working their way along the front row of the high balcony now and she gave a frightened glance toward the stage and saw Jack and Solon standing there talking by the stage light. They must have just appeared since they'd not been there when she and the mad old man had taken the elevator.

"Hold it!" the words came in a shrill voice as Harry popped up ahead of them. He'd been crouching in the dark waiting for them, gun in hand. "You didn't think you'd manage this, did you?" he asked.

Malenkov made no reply. Gale was directly behind him and saw his shoulders firm. In the next second he lunged at the little man. The midget screamed shrilly and fired at him. But nothing halted Malenkov. His hands were around the midget's throat and he crushed it until the evil little face turned purple and both tongue and eyes popped out. Then with a snarl the maddened organist lifted the tiny body and hurled it over the railing.

As Harry went hurtling down into the first balcony pandemonium broke out on the stage. Mavis appeared screaming of their escape. Jack fired a shot up toward the balcony, a futile gesture at the best. And Solon was angrily shouting instructions.

Malenkov was clambering up the steep second balcony steps and she followed after him. She could hear him moaning slightly and was sure that he'd been hit by the bullet Harry had fired.

At the top of the stairs he turned to her and gasped, "Exit over here. To fire escape. It can be forced open. I've tried before."

"Good," she nodded. "Are you hurt?"

"Doesn't matter," he said in the same breathless fashion.

His emaciated face was a grayish white. He stumbled on through a row of seats to the exit door. She was close behind him.

"Now!" he said, as he reached the door. He hurled his bent old body against it with a surprising force. The door creaked and then burst open into the night. She saw that it was foggy and she breathed her first fresh air since she'd entered the old theatre.

"Fire escape dangerous," he told her. "I'll go ahead."

She stepped out on the rusted bars knowing that Solon and the others could reach the balcony any second and she had no time to debate using the precarious method of escape.

"How far down does it go?" she asked.

"To the roof of another building," the old man said. "Hasn't been used for years. Condemned!" He started down, descending into the fog so she could barely see him.

"I'm following," she called. She heard voices, Jack or Solon would be out there after her at any moment.

"Safe so far," Malenkov called up from the foggy depths.

She hastened down, gripping the wet iron rail and feeling it quiver a little. She couldn't see Malenkov as he was quite a long way down. Then the wailing scream came. And she froze and gazed downward in horror. She knew what had happened. Malenkov had fallen!

There was no use calling to him. He was surely a crumpled heap of flesh somewhere in the alley far below. All she could do was find the courage to continue on.

She reached the place where the fire escape had broken away from the building and there was only a gaping void between her and the foggy depths. She had come to the end of the escape route and she was trapped! She had the choice of plunging to her death or becoming a prisoner again.

The choice was never offered her for at that moment Jack reached out and grasped her firmly by the arm. He had gotten down the fire escape to her as she'd crouched there, stunned.

"Too bad," he said, his tone mocking. And he dragged her back up the flimsy fire escape with him. She gave no resistance. She was beyond it. They reached the door to the balcony and he dragged her in.

She expected to see Frank Solon waiting there gloating but he was nowhere in sight. There were shots and shouting from below and she turned to glance at Jack. By the look on his face, he was as surprised as she was by the turn of events.

"Go on," he urged her, pushing her along the aisle roughly.

She stumbled ahead until they reached the rear of the balcony and then from out of the shadows the horror that she had seen so many times before showed itself — the blotched-faced old woman who had haunted her so many midnights. The sight of the phantom was the breaking point. She heard Jack utter an oath as she collapsed.

When she came to, Larry Grant was bent over her. He said, "You're safe. Don't try to figure anything out now."

She stared at him, still dazed. "You?"

"We've taken care of Solon and his gang," the young man said grimly.

"The ghost? She was standing just in front of me!"

"An old woman who used to sing here. She's been living in the cellars as a drunken derelict without anyone knowing."

"Flora Foster?"

"That's her name."

"A ghost! She died!"

"You're wrong there," the young man said. "She's downstairs now and pretty much alive considering her condition. Her death must have been a rumor."

She closed her eyes and moaned. "All of it has been madness!"

"I understand," he agreed.

It was not until later when they sat drinking coffee in the manager's office downstairs that Gale learned the complete story. Larry was a member of the FBI assigned to get evidence against Frank Solon. He'd been working for more than a year on the case without being able to indict the

Mafia man. Then she'd been kidnapped and things began to break. It was the doctor who first talked and divulged the scheme. After that Larry had found it easy to break down her cousin, James Garvis.

"We have Jack and Mavis," the FBI man said grimly. "Solon was shot and killed trying to get out of the theatre. And both Harry and Malenkov are dead. Your cousin and the doctor are already in jail. They'll go on trial along with Jack and Mavis for their share in the murder plot."

She looked up from the chair in which she was seated, her face haggard and sad. "And what about Solon's daughter? Gina?"

Standing before her the young FBI man looked grim. "Poor kid. Perhaps a proper donor will still come along and save her."

"I hope so," she said. "That's what brought it all to a crisis. Frank Solon was determined to have my heart."

Larry's youthful face showed a faint smile. "Out of the question," he said, taking her by the hands and raising her to him, "I already have first claim on it." And he took her in his arms. The nightmare of it all ended in the tenderness of his embrace.

We hope you have enjoyed this Large Print book. Other Thorndike Press or Chivers Press Large Print books are available at your library or directly from the publishers.

For more information about current and upcoming titles, please call or write, without obligation, to:

Thorndike Press
P.O. Box 159
Thorndike, Maine 04986 USA
Tel. (800) 223-1244
Tel. (800) 223-6121

OR

Chivers Press Limited
Windsor Bridge Road
Bath BA2 3AX
England
Tel. (0225) 335336

All our Large Print titles are designed for easy reading, and all our books are made to last.